A Pair of Oars

KERRINA KUHNS

outskirts press

A Pair of Oars

v3.0

Outskirts Press, Inc.
http://www.outskirtspress.com

ISBN: 978-1-9772-5040-7

PRINTED IN THE UNITED STATES OF AMERICA

This book is dedicated to my children for believing in me. I am so grateful for your support and encouragement. Your love means so much. Thanks, bud, for helping me complete a dream.

To my brother Rob, who occasionally whispers in my ear.

To my friend Annie, I can't wait until we can plop down in a beach chair again.

CHAPTER 1

Spirit (spir't): (noun) spiritus, breath, courage, the soul, life, supernatural being.

1842

Charlotte was like any other fisher's wife: strong, hard-working and didn't mind getting her hands dirty. She stood about five feet six inches tall, with dark hair and green eyes. She looked a lot older than she was, life had taken its toll, sometimes taxing her beyond her strength. She had the face of an old Indian squaw, a woman who lived off the land. But the upturned lines on her face reflected spunky confidence, though beaten down a bit. Her hands were not soft but callused, strong, marred by the scars of life. Charlotte spent most of her days and nights alone. Her nights were spent minding the lighthouse at Great Point on Nantucket Island. Her flood of memories started in early 1842 at least that's what she recalled when she felt like she was in her own skin.

The lighthouse was made of stone laid in cement. It was 72 feet high. Years ago, before the fire, it was made of wood but it had been rebuilt. The lamp was lit using the spider lamp method. Four wicks absorbed fuel from whale oil. Charlotte would carry the whale oil supply which was stored at a distance in a protective vault. They were always afraid of another fire. Charlotte wore a veil that covered her nose and mouth to protect her from inhaling smoke.

Though she loved her lighthouse home, Charlotte enjoyed going to town when she could. Minding the lighthouse could be a tiresome, secluded job and anytime she could mingle with the living, well, that was a treat. She enjoyed trips to the local market. She loved the General Store. It was the kind of place where you could get just about all the necessities in one place.

"This light blue fabric with tiny white daisies is just beautiful and would make a wonderful tablecloth. I love daisies. I'll take two yards please."

Down the street, the Market was run by another strong independent woman: Rosie. Oh, don't let the sweet name fool you, Rosie was as sweet as an old fish left out in the sun.

"Good afternoon, Rosie, got any fresh bread today?" Charlotte asked.

Rosie nodded. "Yep, still soft and warm."

Rosie was short and round in a plump, contented way with reddish cheeks and light red hair. Her eyes were brown with dark circles below. Her skin was tan and wrinkled. Her fingers were so caked with flour that she continually wiped her apron. The best bread maker around, they say. The locals called her Rosie. If you called her Rosie to her face, she'd stare at you like death warmed over. Still, deep down she did not mind the nickname from close friends. Charlotte and Rosie were good friends. Together they had experienced more than anyone should endure. They were kindred spirits and would do anything for each other--anything.

"How's the garden going?" Rosie asked.

"Nicely, but I'd like to see what you've got in the way of herbs."

"Sure. Hey, I want to try a new recipe, Char. Might need you to give an opinion,–take a taste or two" Rosie said.

"Of course," Charlotte said, "stop by whenever."

"Well, gotta get back to work."

Twice a month they would meet at the lighthouse for tea.

"See you in a few weeks, girl," Rosie said. "I hope you'll have some honey by then."

Charlotte did the rounds from the market to the local post office across town. You could go months from one letter to the next, but she would check anyway. And she always made it a point to walk the platform known as a widows walk. It was small dock that reached out into the water, waves sloshing below with a gentle splash.

Widows walk could mean many things. Such as the first glimpse of a ship's mast which likely meant loved ones were coming home. It could mean new treasures the likes of which you have never seen before, which included stories you heard rumble through town from men who were fortunate enough to come back across endless waves. These stories would go on for weeks, told over and over, changed by each narrator. It could also mean the loss of a loved one. Charlotte knew the essence of all those scenarios.

The walk back to the Point was one of her favorite things to do. To see the light in the distance was like feeling the beat of her own heart. She loved that old lighthouse, the burden it was and all it stood for. Sometimes she walked along the beach just so she could see it from the outside. She would pick the usual wildflowers. Heck, she didn't care if it was a weed or a flower; if it had color, it was beautiful. She made up stories in her head, wondering where the seeds came from. How far did they fly to land here next to the light?

CHAPTER 2

Low tide: (noun) the time of low water.

Sometime in 2010:

"I have the car loaded," yelled Lilly. "I'm ready to head for the Point, stay out of trouble, would ya?"

"God, it will be great to get out of town," she mumbled.

She hugged her brother, Rob, and gave him a big kiss on the cheek.

"Seriously, stay out of trouble, would you? And figure out a way to quit smoking while I am gone," said Lilly.

Rob was a kind, gentle soul. A large man, dark hair, blue eyes with a kind smile. He could always make Lilly laugh. Lilly enjoyed his visits. Though Rob's recent stroke set him back a bit, he was slowly returning to his normal self. Still, she worried about him.

Lilly was in her mid-forties, and, like most women, needed a change, a freakin break, a change in scenery. She was divorced, her kids grown now—she was a leaf in the wind, just trying to figure out what to do next in life. She was average size, short hair, had been single for over 15 years and was quite comfortable in her own skin. She worked hard at the local oil and gas company sitting at a desk, a desk she was getting bored with.

As she backed out of the driveway, she took a deep breath. She couldn't wait to get on that ferry and breathe in the sea air.

To some, low tide is nothing but wet sand and old seaweed, but to Lilly it was the aroma of peace. To her the sea was calming. The waves had a way of soothing the soul whether slow and calm, or rough and ravaged. She loved all of it. This escape would take her to Nantucket--Great Point to be exact. Her mission was to get started writing her first book. No cell phone, no TV, just her and her laptop, oh, and one of those low folding chairs so she could dig her toes into the beach sand. Also, included in this self-made travel kit, a bottle of wine, along with an old wine glass she grabbed out of the china cabinet.

No plastic wine cups for her—they had to be tinted glass. Nope, she was going in style, gonna make Bette Davis proud.

Finally made it to the ferry. There was something to be said for driving your car onto a boat. She'd always thought a car would be far too heavy for a boat.

Lilly found the perfect place to sit for the long ride. She pulled out her notebook, thinking maybe she could get a few ideas for characters in her book just by people-watching. Looking around, she wondered if these people were looking for an escape as she was. And where was their final destination?

Soon she noticed a woman with her teenage daughter, both dressed like something out of Neiman Marcus. The daughter had the typical look, wearing earphones from the latest I-Pod device while texting, her soul currently sucked into these two devices like she was the only one on the planet. Her mother was trying to talk to her about her studies and asking what the plan was to get her school grades back on track. Of course, her daughter, who was oblivious to what was being said to her, managed to roll her eyes anyway because surely what her mother had to say must be stupid. Suddenly, as if the universe stopped rotating for a brief moment, her mother grabbed her cell phone and hurled it overboard.

Did she just see what she saw? Did she really throw it over the side of the boat into the abyss? Oh, my God, it was awesome—every mother's dream to take control of the damn cell phone from an inconsiderate child. Lilly and the mother gazed at one another, as if they were one spirit, with a cocked smile, a few nods of the head, well done your highness. Nice move. Ah, that was fun even if only an observer. On the other side of the boat was an elderly gentleman who was wearing two different colored tube socks, drinking a cup of coffee in an old N.Y. Giants mug, obviously a true fan. Did they still make tube socks? Unsure that anything was going to top the cell phone episode, she just pulled out a book and relaxed. She soon drove her car off the boat and within minutes saw a beautiful rustic lighthouse.

She settled next to it with a beach chair and was dozing almost immediately. Lily woke to the lap of the incoming tide and the distant sounds of seabirds. The sand dunes had a new look to them this day, as if sometime during the night they decided to dance. The sand under her feet felt heavenly. Walking barefoot was a ritual when she walked the beach. She wondered if this place would look the same in another two hundred and ten years.

CHAPTER 3

Sand [sand]: (noun) moments of time, or of one's life.

Charlotte had been dead for centuries, yet she lived at Great Point stuck in a state she couldn't explain. Friends came and went, yet Charlotte stayed at the same place, watching, and waiting for something she couldn't fathom. She enjoyed the visits from newcomers and from the faithful, those who came year after year to reap the joys of the Great Point, at least that's what she told herself. The spirits knew that if you visited Great Point there was a woman there to guide you. This year she would encounter an experience like nothing ever before.

Charlotte sat on the sand dunes feeling the breeze blowing about her, the sand crusted between her toes. She pulled up her weathered dress to feel the sun on her skin.

"Hello, Char, it's Rosie coming for the monthly cup of tea."

"Sit down, Rosie, enjoy the salt air with me for a bit. I wonder who will visit us this year?"

"God, I hope it's not those same kids who came last year, you know, the ones who left trash all about the place. What was that one child named? Spike. Who names their child Spike? What kind of foolish name is that? He has a mean streak to him, Char, he needed a good whooping with a paddle. What say if those children come again, we plan a ghost sighting?"

A ghost sighting was pure enjoyment for Charlotte and Rosie; they could spend hours planning a masterful event. For them it was a well-planned script that had to be just right to leave the viewers thinking. But sometimes they would just leave well enough alone. They had to be careful not to mess with their heads.

"Don't want to ruin them for life," Char would say. "Most important we don't want the Point to become a circus for every nut case who thought they knew all about so-called spirits."

Even though Char and Rosie were spirits they could feel things, things at the Point like sand, wind, and cold. Every so often they found items washed up on shore, things they did not recognize, things they would love to have. They collected items like sea glass, starfish, shells, and faded pages from newspapers. Char loved the sea glass because she knew at some point there might have been something fabulous held within its shape.

"Rosie, you ready for some tea?"

"Sure am."

The best place to have tea was atop the lighthouse. Up there you could see forever on either side of the island. Char and Rosie's tea would take place at a small table, a bit wobbly at times. The table was covered with a handmade lace tablecloth with a few stains. Char loved this tablecloth. It reminded her of the old days, shopping in the market where she purchased the table linen. The tea pot was Rosie's, a pot handed down from her mother. Light blue with millions of tiny cracks, sort of a character of its own. If the pot could talk it would have a lot of stories to share of women and all their gossipy tales.

"Wish I could fix that old chip," Rosie would say every time the pot was out.

"Ah, I like the old chip," Char said.

"Wouldn't look the same if you could fix it."

Rosie would place the small broken piece next to the pot as if it had to be a part of the pot whether sitting next to it or attached to it.

"What kinda tea we got today, Char?"

"Today, it's mint tea."

Mint tea was the last tea she purchased in the market. It would be the last thing she would purchase, period, as a live human being. On the table, beside the tea pot, a candle was strategically placed. Sometimes they lit three or four candles just because they enjoyed the ambiance; the flicker of the light made them feel alive.

"What's that over there?" Char said.

"Looks like a woman walking toward the lighthouse."

"At this time of night, the sun will be going down and the tide rolling in," Rosie replied. What she gonna do here now?"

CHAPTER 4

*Lighthouse [**lahyt**-hous]: (noun) a tower or other structure displaying or flashing a very bright light for the guidance of ships in avoiding dangerous areas, in following certain routes, etc.*

Lilly checked into the hotel right on the harbor. She dragged her luggage up the steep narrow stairs and found her way to the room. It was small but cozy and had a small green couch with a coffee table, a side chair, a four-post bed, and a charming bathroom off to the side. The best part of the room was the balcony. It had just enough room to step out on and take in the view of the harbor. Boats were everywhere, some small, some larger than her house. Good grief.

Who lived in that floating hotel over there? Unbelievable! She stretched her neck so that she could peek in the window. The boat docked just a few yards from the balcony. Inside was a very large TV, a sitting area that looked like something out of Forbes magazine. She could only imagine the cost to keep one of those afloat.

Lilly was starving after the long drive and decided to ask the front desk for a good place to eat close by. The young man, who could not be more than eighteen, told her that down the street was a pizza place, best pizza in town. Perfect. He was right.

The next day Lilly drove to the Point. She was anxious to again see the lighthouse she had read about but mostly she wanted to get her feet in the sand. After she parked, she headed out. The wind whipped her hair. It was chilly enough to don a sweater. The sea air was invigorating. The the damp sand, the wind, all of it was what she needed to escape the humdrum of everyday life. After collecting a few seashells, Lilly sat in one spot for hours, as if she needed to memorize everything and store it in the back of her mind, savor it when she might need it later. Hours later she realized it was getting late, but she was lost in the feeling.

She wished she could get up to the top of the lighthouse. Bet the view was awesome from up there. She began to walk around the tall structure placing her hand on the stone, cement wall as if to feel it breathing. It was a strong lighthouse, and looked proud to be here.

Lilly stopped and turned around, feeling as if she was being watched, raising her hand above her eyes to block the setting sun, looking for something or someone. Realizing it would be dark soon, she decided to head back to the car. She carried her bag of shells as if she had found some great prize, cradling them in her arms so as to not disturb their current form. She was enjoying the gentle breezes. Again, she glanced back as if she was being watched.

CHAPTER 5

Kindred spirit: (noun) also kindred soul. An individual with the same beliefs, attitudes or feeling as oneself.

Today Charlotte was watching the sunrise on the horizon and noticed the wind blowing more than usual. She loved it when the wind blew, it meant change was coming. As she leaned up against the lighthouse, enjoying all the gifts the beach had to offer she noticed a newspaper blowing across the beach. Oh, my God, a paper. She rushed over to see if she could grab it. Maybe, she could see what the date is, and maybe, just maybe, read something that was happening in the world. She felt like a child trying to catch the ice cream truck. Luckily, the paper got snagged against some tall green grass with the grass blowing and bending as if to say, "I got it." Charlotte hovered over the paper holding her hand out in front to see if her body would let her grasp it. She reached out quickly before the wind took the paper. Off it went into the breeze. Again, it was caught by some tall sea grass.

"Shoot!" she said out loud. "I wonder what the date is?"

As the corner of the paper flipped back and forth, she saw June 10, 2010. Wow, 2010. It had been almost five years since she'd seen a date on a newspaper. The paper was weathered from the elements, yellowed, and torn. It was the obituary section. Charlotte leaned back. How ironic that it was the obituary section. Just a cruel joke from her so-stuck life. She tried to grab hold of the paper again but just as quickly as it came, the wind took it away again high into the sky. The paper waved as if it was saying goodbye. Well, at least the paper didn't blow into the water. She hated trash in the water.

Charlotte and Rosie roamed the small lighthouse island. As spirits, both had been dead for many years. But even in death, they were still kindred spirits. They had the ability to come and go, see things and people. Sometimes they could pick up items. Other times items would sift through their fingers; they were not sure why. They often met other spirits who passed through on the way to nowhere. They could also mingle among the living, Rosie's favorite kind of adventure.

Charlotte lost her husband, Henry, many years ago. When he died, she did not know. Childhood sweethearts they were. Henry was tall, with dark hair he pulled back in a ponytail. Hazel eyes like sea glass. He had a small scar across his face from a wild fishing hook. He would tell the children in town he got it from wrestling pirates while looking for buried treasure and then he'd pull a coin out of his pocket --a coin he himself found one day while fishing. The coin was large, gold, and was so worn you could not make out what was stamped on it. It looked like it was a hundred years old. The children would ask to hold the coin as if they could sense the tale it could tell if it could talk.

Henry left on a Tuesday morning. He loaded his gear as usual. He and Charlotte walked together while the sun rose.

"Remember to close things up tight when hurricane season comes, Char," he told her.

"I know, same as every year, Henry. I promise I will make sure the boards are secure on the windows."

"You remember where I keep the nails, right?"

"Same place as always, don't worry, I'll take care of everything including your garden."

Henry loved to work the land. They had a small garden planted on the other side of the lighthouse, encircled by a rock wall. Protected from the heavy winds. Henry would say, "Hands in the water, are good for the spirit, and hands in the dirt are good for the soul." He loved the garden and all it gave him. He appreciated the wonder of a small seed and what it might become.

As they neared the small town, Char started to get that tight feeling in the back of her throat fighting the urgent tears.

"How long do you think you'll be gone this time?" she asked.

"Oh, maybe three to six months, not sure yet," he replied. There were numerous factors that would determine when a ship returned, such as the success of the catch, bad weather, sickness, or a battered ship in need of repair. The town understood these things. Henry boarded the Anibell, named after the captain's sister. After he had all his gear loaded, he walked off the boat to say goodbye.

Henry lifted both his hands and held Charlotte's face as he leaned in to kiss her. His hands felt rough, warm, and comforting all at the same time. Then he held her tight in his arms as she clung to his lapels. Tears ran down her cheeks as she tried to be strong.

"Maybe this time, Char, I will bring you back a beautiful ruby or sapphire stone ring," he said as he lifted her left hand, rubbing it gently.

Char smiled. "Just come back, that's all I need."

They kissed again and held each other, feeling the wind wrap around them, joining in the farewell.

Charlotte would not get on the widow's walk until the Anibell was off in the distance; it was a tradition to wait until you could barely see the top of the mast. As she stood on the walk, below her feet came noises of wood grinding against wood, sloshing of small waves. Char lifted her hand to her cheek, savoring the memory of Henry's hand against her face.

"Please come back," she whispered in the wind, hoping the message would carry across the sea. "Please come back to me."

CHAPTER 6

Thalassophile: (noun) a lover of the sea, someone who loves the sea, ocean.

Lilly was up early and could not wait to feel the sting of the sand blowing against her body. She put on her favorite sweater, a kind of a cream color that went down past her hips with big chunky buttons. It looked like she bought it from the Hamptons. She loved it. Adding a pair of jeans and sandals, Lilly packed up her laptop, notebook, and pencil. One stop at the market and she could get a nice picnic together. Bottled water, a sandwich and some beautiful grapes sounded good today. She decided to bring a small bottle of wine. The market was buzzing with people getting ready for the day. After shopping, she jumped into the car and drove to the nearest spot to make the hike up to the Point.

She hoped no one was up there today, it would be great to take it all in with no interruptions and no distractions. Perfect. Hers was the only car in the parking lot, at least for now. The tricky part was the skill needed to carry her laptop bag, picnic basket and chair without falling over.

"I can do this," she said.

Lilly slipped the strap of the bag over her head on one side and then slipped the folded chair over the other side, looking like an armed professional beach tourist and then picked up her basket but not before slipping off her sandals and sticking them in the back of her pants pocket.

"I got this," she said, "but I look like a dork."

She made her way along the shore to the Great Point. Lilly had to stop a few times to readjust her equipment and stretch her hands. Finally, she found a spot between two sand dunes, thinking maybe she might be a bit protected from the sea wind but close enough to the lighthouse to enjoy its comfort and security.

Once she got her chair situated in the right spot, she plopped down to enjoy the view. It was sunny with shifting winds. Off in the distance she could see some gray clouds, the kind that might hold a few raindrops. She didn't care, she was finally where she wanted to be.

"God, it feels good," she said and rolled up her jeans a bit so she could take full advantage of the sun on her skin. Once settled in she pulled out her laptop. Opening a blank word document, she took a deep breath and waited for some insight. She raised her hands in front of the monitor.

"What's it gonna be, girl?" she said. "I can't believe how happy I am just sitting here."

CHAPTER 7

Laptop [lap-top]: (noun) a portable computer, usually battery-powered, small enough to rest in the user's lap, having a screen that closes over the keyboard like a lid.

Charlotte noticed a woman sitting on the beach and couldn't wait to get over to her. As a spirit, she could move about the lighthouse quickly, but she would rather walk. Made her feel like she was still alive. Approaching like she was receiving a mystery gift, she leaned over Lilly's shoulder, slowly with caution. She had seen this thing before, once when a young man came for a while, but he did not stay long enough for her to figure out what it was. Lilly reached up to rub her neck as if she could feel something. She turned her head, looking about with a perplexed expression, like she was being watched.

"Huh," she said. "What is it about this place?"

Why did she have such a strange feeling? Lilly typed the date on the keyboard and where she was.

Char began growing excited. I get it; you punch the keys and viola it shows up on the picture thing. Instantly Char wanted to see if she could hit a button. She must try it—she just had to hit one of those buttons. She needed to do this gracefully so as not to spook this woman. Slowly she reached over Lilly's shoulder and hit a "K." There it was plain as day on the picture screen. She leaned back, clasping her hands together in pure joy.

Lilly looked back at the screen after gazing over the sea.

"How'd that get there?" she said aloud, quickly hitting the backspace key. Just like that the "K' was gone and just like that Char became deflated at what she had done. Lilly again began to feel like she was being watched. She stood up, set the laptop on her beach chair, and put her hands on her hips as she gazed across the beach in all directions. She wondered if someone was in the lighthouse. She took a few steps in that direction, looking for anyone.

"Anyone there?" she yelled, no response. Taking a few more steps she yelled again. Then she made her way back to the chair and lifted her laptop back onto her lap. There was the word "C-H-A-R-L-O-T-T-E" on the screen. Startled, she jumped up out of the chair and looked around.

"Okay, this is freaking me out," she said. She looked for footsteps in the sand, a fast getaway, someone hiding close by.

"I know I did not type this and who is Charlotte anyway?"

Charlotte stood there in awe. Finally, after all these years she had a connection with the living. Her mind became abuzz. She felt alive again. Oh God, she was breaking her own rule to not change the life of a living human being. She needed to think about this, maybe talk to Rosie, see what she might think.

Just then Charlotte saw a dog walking down the beach. She could tell it was a spirit dog right away. The dog had beautiful golden reddish blond hair and was clearly enjoying her walk along the beach. Char felt it was important to visit with the spirits. They would always pass through, and some would return, while others she wouldn't see again. She could never figure out why she just stayed at the lighthouse.

Char reached down to pet the beautiful retriever, discovering there was a collar with a name, Pepper. "Pepper," she said aloud.

"Well, hello Pepper and welcome to Great Point. You're welcome to stay if you like. My name is Charlotte, Char for short." The two went walking along the beach as if they'd known each other for years. Pepper led the way while occasionally stopping to investigate something, but then quickly bolted to get ahead of Char, brushing her leg as she flew by. A couple of times she almost knocked Char down in her attempts to be first on their walk. Pepper stopped and sat down in the sand, panting to catch her breath, then finally lay down wiggling in the sand to get a good back scratch. She flipped her body around a few times making her impression in the sand just right, so she could rest. Once Char caught up, she plopped down next to Pepper. She could tell in Pepper's eyes that she'd been loved.

"I bet there is family out there missing you, huh?" she said. Pepper lifted her head and looked at Charlotte as if saying "yes, and I miss them too." The two sat there for a long time. Char knew it was important to make the spirits that came by feel welcome, knowing each one had a story. If she visited with them, she might hear what was going on in the world, but most of all she could, in some way, let them know everything would be okay for them.

Rosie showed up. "Oh, my goodness, how long has it been since we've had a visit from a dog, Char?"

"Her name is Pepper, that's what it says here on her tag."

"Pepper, I love it. Oh, Char, do you think she'll stay with us?"

"Don't know, guess we'll have to wait and see." Rosie reached out to touch Pepper's beautiful fur.

"Hello, puppy," Rosie said. The three of them sat watching the waves roll in and out, just enjoying each other. Charlotte had briefly forgotten about Lilly and what she had done, the buttons she pushed.

CHAPTER 8

Oars (or) noun; a long pole with a broad blade at one end, held in place by an oarlock and used in pairs to row a boat.

BACK IN 1842.

Charlotte and Rosie decided to take out the boat. It was a small boat named Charlotte Rose. Henry named her and at times he'd talk to her like an old friend. The name was painted on the boat with refinement. The oars were handmade by Henry. Just the thought of holding the oars made Char feel a part of him. Every time she picked up the oars, she'd run her hands up and down the wood to find connection in the grain. She knew the place for the perfect grip on the oars, due to Henry's constant instruction.

"Hold it in the groove, hold tight," he would say. Charlotte looked out at the water and whispered, "Please come back to me." Just then a gust of wind flew round about her body.

"Got my pole," Rosie exclaimed out loud, "you got the basket, Char?"

"Yes, right here, brought us some of that good bread and cheese too."

"I couldn't help but notice you admiring those oars," Rosie said. "Like you were talking to someone. Char, you okay?"

"Yes, just thinking about when Henry made these from that old oak tree, is all," said Char.

"Well, let's get out there before the tide changes on us and we get heat stroke trying to get out in the big blue," Rosie said.

They jumped into the small boat like seasoned boaters. For some reason Char and Rosie began to giggle like little girls out on an adventure.

"Well, that was real lady like," exclaimed Rosie.

"One of these days we gotta build us a nice dock so we can get into this boat without getting wet as a cod."

Char got a big smile on her face, "What fun that would be."

"Please, we ain't no ladies in waiting or something," said Rosie.

Rosie would always row out first, she had more strength to get past the waves rolling in to meet land than Char. Char never gave her instructions about using the oars. Rosie knew how important they were to her--not to mention she knew what she was doing better than Char did. Besides, if one of them dropped an oar they knew they'd be swimming back to shore. Which could be exhausting to say the least. Soon they were out on a more settled sea.

"Ah, the sweet sound of sloshing waves," Rosie said.

"I say we head over around the cove and sit a spell, somewhere we have not been in a while."

Off in the distance Char could see Old Man Roberts, a tall black man waving.

"Good luck, ladies," he yelled.

Old Man Roberts could catch a fish with his eyes closed, one arm tied behind his back, and the other arm in a sling. The townspeople would ask him advice based on his fishing skills. He liked to tell stories. He convinced the children that he and the critters of the sea were brother and sister, and they could talk to each other. He also knew when a big storm was coming. If he told you to close shop and batten down, you did what he said. Mr. Robert's weakness--getting drunk on any given day.

"Char, does it look like he has his teeth in today?" asked Rosie.

"Yep, sure does," Char said, waving back to Mr. Roberts. "Hope he saved some fish for us."

Charlotte was looking out in the distance as if searching for something.

"Rosie, it kinda feels creepy out here today. Do you feel it?"

"Ah, it's a beautiful day today, lots of sunshine, stiff breeze," Rosie said as she looked out to sea.

Hours passed and neither had caught a fish. "What's going on down there, I wonder?" said Rosie.

"I'm telling you, something feels creepy today. I can't explain it," Char said, glancing around.

"Let's take a break and try some of that bread and cheese you brought," said Char.

"I must say, this batch of bread I made has been the best so far this year," said Rosie. "I think last night I ate a whole loaf by myself."

"Your bread is always good," replied Char. "One of these days you're going to let me make some with you, right?"

"Now, you know it's a family recipe, girl."

"Well, ain't I family?" Char snapped back with a half-smile on her face.

"You know I love ya, Char, but my bread, it's like all I got left of family." The two women looked up at each other and started laughing.

"We'll, we better get the Charlotte Rose back in before the tide gets too high. "The fish must have declared this day a fast!"

"What's that noise?" Char leaned over the side of the boat.

"You hear that? Sounds like the water is churning out in the middle of nowhere."

Rosie looked out the other side, "I hear it too."

The small boat began to shift and move as if it was being pulled side to side. Within minutes a hole, like a large funnel opened up. The water became more and more turbulent. The hole grew bigger and bigger. The churning noise was louder and louder like a surge of water being sucked into a drain. Panic struck, Rosie pulled on the oars in an effort to row away from the twisting water. Its strength was beyond anything Rosie had experienced. Something dark was pulling them. The spray of water began to strike their faces like darts from the sea. Rosie struggled to get the boat to move in another direction, any direction away from the large, deep hole that was getting closer and closer. They could now see down in the dark abyss. Char said, "Let me, Rosie," she moved next to Rosie and grabbed an oar, but her shaking hands could not hold onto one of her prized possessions and in a quick snap, the oar was gone, sucked into the water as if someone below had snatched it out of her hands.

"No," yelled Char as the boat lurched into the large hole, dipping sideways before it tipped over.

Rosie and Char were pulled down in the cold, icy water. Their dresses were wrapped so tightly against their bodies, their struggles only made the cloth tighter. Char tried to keep Rosie in her sight, but she was disoriented and panicked. Soon she saw mountains, underwater, with huge ledges. Violent water. Another world existed close to her lighthouse. Where was Rosie, oh, God, where was her beloved Rosie. Then, instant black darkness.

CHAPTER 9

*Whirlpool [**hwurl**-pool, **wurl**]: (noun) water in swift, circular motion, as that produced by the meeting of opposing currents, often causing a downward spiraling action.*

Charlotte found herself sitting on the beach. She knew she was dead but remained a spirit on earth. How long it had been since their innocent boat ride, she did not know. Would she ever see Rosie? Was Rosie alive or a spirit like her? Char didn't know what to do. Everything seemed lighter, carefree, yet a bit lonely. Something caught her eye down the beach. She jumped up, started running, shouting, "Hello? Hello!" all while waving her arms. Soon she realized it was Rosie. Char threw her arms around her.

"Are you dead, too, Rosie?"

"Dead as a doornail," she replied. Char burst into tears.

"I am so sorry. It's all my fault. We should have never gone out on the boat. I knew it. Something felt wrong out there. I knew it," she yelled as she paced back and forth on the sand. "Will you ever forgive me?"

"Settle down, girl, there is nothing to forgive. We did everything together. Hell, I can't think of another person I'd rather drown with," replied Rosie.

"They just stood there in awe of each other, then sat

down on a soft sand dune for hours trying to grasp what had happened.

Char looked over at Rosie. "You look a little thinner, Rosie. I think this dead thing suits you." They burst out in laughter.

"Maybe that's because I was trying to swim out of the whirlpool that would not let go while trying to save that damned oar of yours," said Rosie. They leaned against each other, sitting, taking it all in.

CHAPTER 10

*Sweater [**swet**-er]: (noun) a knitted or crocheted outer garment, in pullover or cardigan style.*

Lilly could not sleep all night, thinking about what had appeared on her laptop, she knew she had to get back to the Point. The sun was rising when Lilly jumped out of bed. She did her usual jaunt down to the lobby for a cup of coffee and a crescent roll to start the day. Back at the Point parking lot, she loaded up the usual gear. She walked to the same spot she visited yesterday, close to the lighthouse. As she walked, she was talking aloud.

"I'm gonna pay more attention to that lighthouse, someone could be in there." She wondered if this could be the start of her new book.

She plopped down all her stuff, looked around–no one in sight. She loved it, the whole beach to herself. The chair was set just right, the notebook was handy, the laptop good to go, as was the fancy water bottle purchased from the lobby. She opened a new blank document, still looking around as if someone would appear at any moment. She waited.

"This is ridiculous, snap out of it and get to a plan, a cover page, something, woman!" she said loudly. She planted her feet firmly in the sand, took a deep breath, felt the sun on her face.

Charlotte was off in the distance. Ah, the lady with the button thing was back. Charlotte moved and stood behind Lilly, admiring the color of her hair. She had a familiar smell, lavender. She admired Lilly's beautiful dark brown sweater, wishing she could try it on. She noticed Lilly's jewelry, a square-shaped locket with leaf designs on the front. Lilly's ring was silver with a large pearl-like stone, brown, almost like her sweater. Lilly's eyes were emerald green–an aura of kindness, a gentle soul. She had a good feeling about her.

Lilly again felt as if she was being watched; again, she stood up from her chair and said, "Is anyone there?" Within a few minutes she sat down again.

Charlotte was excited. Never before had anyone paid attention to her. Could this woman feel her presence? Could she see her? Charlotte reached out and touched Lilly's arm to calm her.

As if she was in a dream, Lilly began to see a silhouette of Charlotte, a sort of cloudy formation of a woman. Startled, Lilly backed away, tipping over in her beach chair.

"Oh my God, what is happening to me?" Lilly put her hands over her face, knees still in the sand.

"Can you see me; can you really see me?" cried Charlotte. "I'm Charlotte. Charlotte is my name." She reached out to touch Lilly again. Tears ran down her face, hands trembled. "Can you see me?"

"I'm Lilly, I don't understand. Are you a ghost?" Lilly stood up, glancing around to see if anyone was nearby.

"I'd like to think of myself as a spirit of sorts," said Charlotte. "I have been here at the Point since 1845, well, even before that since I grew up here, but I drowned out there." Charlotte pointed off in the distance. She had never said those words to anyone before, the words came out as if they were in slow motion, as if she was experiencing a rite of passage. It just felt weird saying the words aloud.

"Tell me, what is the year, what year are you living in?" asked Charlotte.

"It's 2010," Lilly replied.

Charlotte dropped down in the sand. "Yes, I think I remember seeing that date on an old newspaper. I can't imagine what the world is like now," she said. They stared at each other as if neither could believe what they were seeing.

"Lilly, have you ever been here before?"

"Never," Lilly said.

"I came here to the Point because I needed inspiration to write a book. I have always wanted to write a book and I love the ocean so I thought if I could just sit here maybe I would get inspired. I was here yesterday, and it felt as if someone was watching me, was that you?"

"Yes," said Charlotte, "I watched you but never thought I'd see you again, let alone have a conversation with you. I see folks come and go year after year; some I never see again and some I remember from another time. I also visit with other spirits. It's the same thing. Some I see over and over and others only once. I have yet to figure out why. Rosie and I are the only ones who seem to stay."

"Who is Rosie?" asked Lilly.

"Rosie is my best friend. We did everything together. We even drowned together."

"Is Rosie here now?"

"No, I haven't seen her all day, but she will show up. I don't know if you'll be able to see her, too. She is just going to spit when she hears about you."

"I'm not even sure what's happening here," Lilly said. She felt like she was losing it. The two women sat in the sand looking at each other. Occasionally they'd reach out to each other and touch just for reassurance.

Lilly asked Charlotte, "May I touch your hands?"

Charlotte reached out her hands, palms up. Lilly laid her hands on top of Charlotte's hands. It felt cool with a slight feeling of a piece of cotton cloth–soothing. Lilly noticed Char's hands looked like the hands of someone who had worked hard.

Lilly asked Charlotte, "How does it feel to you?"

"Your hands are warm; they feel a little heavy. I love that they are tan from the sun, something I remember from when I was alive, like leather. I used to love the feeling of the sun on my skin. I don't feel that anymore, but I remember it like it was yesterday." She closed her eyes and lifted her face to the sky.

"Will you be here for a while?" Charlotte asked. "Will you come again?"

"Yes," Lilly responded.

"Do you think we will see each other again?"

"I hope so," said Lilly. "I'd better walk back to my car before it's too dark." Lilly was thinking she might see a ghost on the way out. She would not dare say it out loud since she was not sure what was happening.

"If you don't mind, Lilly, may I walk with you?" asked Charlotte.

"Sure, wish you could help carry some stuff."

"Sorry, I haven't mastered that yet. Wish I could try on that sweater, she said with a slight smile.

The two women walked side by side wondering what was happening and why it was happening now, and why to each other?

CHAPTER 11

*Library [**lahy**-brer-ee]: (noun) a place set apart to contain books, periodicals, and other material for reading, viewing, listening, study, or reference, as a room, set of rooms, or building where books may be read or borrowed.*

Lilly barely got any sleep thinking about her encounter on the beach. How could she see Charlotte when no one else could? Before she knew it, the sun was coming up. She quickly jumped out of bed, got dressed and headed over to the archive library. The temperature was brisk.

"A scarf is a must," she said to herself.

The library was small and dark. The walls were lined with large, yellowed books. As Lilly gazed about the room, she could not help but wonder how many books lined these vintage walls. It smelled like an old museum with old furniture. Old but beautiful pieces hugged the walls. Lilly was like a kid in a candy store, excited to dive in.

To the side of the room sat an elderly man with gray hair, glasses balancing on the tip of his nose. He wore a worn flannel shirt, the kind Paul Bunyan must have worn. This guy was so old he looked as if he'd grown roots right there in the chair.

"How can I help you, honey?" he said.

Instantly Lilly felt his kindness.

"Ah, I'm not sure where to start. I am researching, maybe newspaper articles from the 1840s. Specifically a drowning, a drowning of two women off Great Point."

"Okay, well you'd better start with a cup of coffee over there because you may be here awhile."

Lilly took a deep breath and filled a cup, adding sugar and cream.

"Coffee makes everything marvelous," she said.

The elderly man stuck out his hand

"My name is Harry Blum, but you can call me Harry."

"Nice to meet you, I'm Lilly." Funny, Lilly noticed Harry's hands looked just like Charlotte's hands, worn, calloused and almost translucent. Harry led Lilly to the back corner where there was a rough wood table and several mismatched chairs. Something you might see in a country school.

"You will have plenty of space and privacy here," said Harry. "I have to admit, I haven't had a good research project in a while so I hope you will let me help you. I'm sure we will become good friends in the process. Let me know when you'll be back, I'll bring you some of my wife's homemade pumpkin cookies, best in the world."

"I love anything pumpkin," said Lilly.

Harry pointed to a book bonded in dark leather.

"Start here, Lilly, while I help the gentleman who just walked in."

"Of course, thank you," she said.

Lilly opened the large book, the pages crinkling as she carefully turned each sheet. Her thoughts began to flow. She wondered when was the last time someone looked through these pages. The newspaper was titled The Great Point News, the dates were hard to read in tiny black print. She decided to get out her old lady glasses. Each paper was not lengthy, but she was enjoying the small stories of the community food market, items for sale, the latest events at the local fair, who caught the biggest fish, popular fabric to make dresses, the pie contest, the local drunk. Most intriguing were the stories of ships, what cargo they brought in. What happened to ships that did not return within the expected time frame. Lilly was getting lost in the times.

"These people truly lived," she whispered. It seemed like the community was alive. Thriving together. Day to day tasks were necessities to survive. Handmade tools, passed down to generations. There were no distractions like cell phones and fancy appliances.

"They worked hard, but they lived a simple life."

Some of the pages had wrinkles in the middle. The wrinkles absorbed words like a canyon in time.

"Gotta be really careful with these pages, so I don't ruin anything," she whispered leaning in to take a deep whiff of the book. Then she leaned back in the old chair, took a sip of coffee, and thought for a moment about Charlotte. It would be cool to sit here with her. She could tell all about her life, like friends flipping through an old photo album.

God, this coffee was good. Lilly snuggled up with her scarf and went back to the old book.

Harry returned with an eager look on his face

"How are we doing over here? Do you mind telling me about what you're trying to research?" he asked.

Lilly had to think quickly, she certainly did not dare tell him the truth.

"I need to write a story for a creative writing class I'm taking. Once I had read something brief about two women off the Point who had drowned. I thought that could be the start of an interesting story" she said. She hoped he couldn't tell she was lying. She was not a good liar.

Harry looked at her for a moment, pushing his glasses up on his nose and resting his hand on his hips. "Well, alright then."

CHAPTER 12

Tea [te]: (noun) a reception or other social gathering in the afternoon, at which the tea, coffee, are served.

Charlotte waited in her favorite place in the lighthouse. It was a room just below the lantern room. The lantern room enclosed the light and the lens, surrounded by a catwalk. Just below the catwalk was another room. This room had large windows where you could watch all the activities on the water. It was a small room, but cozy. The windows were thick, old, beaten by the wind. Charlotte was hoping Lilly would show up again. Maybe she spooked her. She still didn't understand: why was this woman different? Hopefully she would come back.

Char waited impatiently for Rosie. It was tea day, and she couldn't wait to tell Rosie about the encounter. The wind was blowing pretty hard, it might signal a change in the weather. Char stood on top at the old lighthouse, her dress blowing like a flag, hands gripping the catwalk railing as she had done a thousand times. The clouds were coming fast; white caps were building. She could see them off in the distance like a flock of seagulls swarming toward the shore. Though she knew there were no whaling boats out there she would look anyway, squinting her eyes to make sure she was not missing anything.

Soon Rosie showed up with the tea of the day.

"Change is in the air, huh?" said Rosie.

"Yep, something's brewing today," said Char.

"Let's get out of the wind, don't want my special vanilla tea to blow away, and this wind messes up my hair." They both laughed.

Char spoke up quickly, "Rosie, you are not going to believe what happened yesterday."

"I know. I was watching you," Rosie said.

"You were there? Why did you not say something?"

"I didn't know what to think. I was a bit spooked myself."

Char leaned forward sitting up straight in her chair. "Since when are you spooked?"

"Char, we been here for how long and all of a sudden this woman can see you?" asked Rosie.

"I needed a sip of some of Henry's homemade brew to ponder over all this."

"What? You still have some?" Char snapped back.

"Not much left and tastes a bit powerful—just enough to snap me back into my skin," Rosie said. "Well, if a dead person can do that... I don't know, but it hits you like a ton of bricks."

Char looked at her and said, "Well, how does it taste in hot tea?" The two women burst out laughing like girls' night out.

"I'd say we are in for some excitement," said Rosie as she poured Char some tea.

"It's about damn time, huh."

There came a spirit down the beach, a small, frail-looking woman wrapped in free-flowing white cloth. She wore a headdress that had approximately a two-inch width strip and two smaller stripes that framed her face. The stripes also lined the edge of the fabric that crossed her chest. On her top left shoulder was a pin in the shape of a cross. She walked with a bit of a lean forward; her face was gripping. Charlotte and Rosie headed toward her. She had an aura surrounding her like no other spirit they had seen before. The wrinkles on her face were like the bark of a willow tree, each line deep but graceful. Her eyes were big and looked as though the lids were heavy. Her smile was that of simplicity and selflessness; she was beautiful. Once the women were in front of each other the small woman greeted them by placing her hands together in front of her with a slight bow of the head.

"Hello," said Charlotte and Rosie, "we are having tea. Would you like to join us?"

She said, "I would love to," in a slight accent. The conversation that followed was about the many people the small woman had met on earth, as well as ones in heaven. Char and Rosie could tell the woman's life consisted of nothing but kindness with a giving heart.

"Have you been by here before?" asked Charlotte.

"No," she replied as she looked out over the water.

"It certainly is beautiful, and I love the smell of the tide. How long have you been here?"

"We are not sure, but we don't go anywhere else and don't know why," said Char. "We see other spirits who come and go, we even see the living."

The small woman finished her tea, thanked her hostesses, stood up and said simply, "Maybe you are here for a reason; maybe there is unfinished work to be done, or maybe someone's soul needs your touch."

The small woman pondered for a moment. Her hands clasped together, in front of her small chest.

She asked, "Is there a living keeper of the lighthouse?"

Char and Rosie were still overcome by this woman's presence and felt what she had to say was important.

"Maybe I will come back and visit you and see how you're doing," she said.

"We would like that," said Char. "Forgive us but we have sat here all this time and don't even know what your name is."

She said, "Teresa, God bless you," and she was gone.

"You feel goose bumps, Char?" said Rosie. "She got some kind a power, that one."

"I hope she comes back," said Char, "she also carries with her a kind of peace, she's a good soul."

CHAPTER 13

Wind; n. air in motion; a strong, fast moving, or destructive natural current of air; gale or storm

Lilly decided to head for the Point, just to check and see if she was crazy. The wind was really rough today. She supposed there was no point in doing her hair this morning. She took her shoes off, it being too hard to walk on the sand with her Converse on. Lilly sat down on the soft sand and untied her shoes. As she pulled the shoelaces she looked out toward the sea. God, she could never get tired of this place. The waves were huge today and appeared higher where she was sitting. A quick jump up and she headed toward the lighthouse.

Charlotte standing there, clear as day with only a bit of a silhouette, luminous and beautiful.

"Hi, Charlotte," Lilly said.

"Hello, I wasn't sure if I would ever see you again. I thought you might be scared or maybe you were like some of the others we see here; they come and go, and we never see them again."

"We?" said Lilly, "anyone else here with you? I can't see anyone else."

Lilly leaned over to look beyond Char, gazing in both directions.

"Right now, it's just you and me, but Rosie might be by later."

"Rosie was the one with you in the boat, right?" Lilly was searching for more information so she could do better research at the library. Lilly decided to confess her library research. Lilly was dying to ask personal questions, like when did they die? Reluctant, since they had just met, she held off. The two women sat down on the side of a sand drift to protect themselves from the forceful wind.

Char noticed Lilly's shoes beside the woman. "Aren't those shoes a bit odd for a woman to be wearing?"

Lilly said, "Yeah, but they're really comfortable, you want to try them on? Go ahead."

Char reached over to pick up the shoe. She was excited in anticipation, wondering whether she'd be able to feel the shoe on her foot. She slipped her foot inside the shoe, it was a bit loose, but she stood up and walked a few feet.

"What do you think? How do they look?" Char asked with a grin on her face.

"Groovy," said Lilly "they look great."

"They are comfortable. I don't think I've ever had a comfortable shoe before.

"Luckily, I do like walking around on the sand in my bare feet. It makes me feel like I'm part of the living."

"Charlotte, I need to confess. I went to the library to see if I could find some information on you and Rosie and the day you died. Do you mind?"

"No, not at all. I would love to hear what was written about that day myself."

"There is a nice man there, Harry Blum. He's the librarian who is helping me and seems to be just as excited as I am."

"Does the library still smell like old wood?" Char asked.

A grin formed on her face. "Yep, still smells old," said Lilly. "The sloping wood floors make that creaky noise. It's kinda cool knowing we were both at the same place even though it was at different times."

Lilly decided to ask a few questions. "Can you go anywhere else or just here by the lighthouse?"

Char sighed, "It seems like I stay here but several times I've gone into town. I'm not sure how but sometimes I find myself walking along the streets, mostly late at night. The town has really changed. Definitely a lot more going on than during my life. There are lots of people, it's exciting. Sometimes I lean up against the bookstore window. I never seen so many books in one place and I wonder what are they all about."

Lilly said, "You should see the library. It has tons of books and tons of history. It's amazing."

"What about that box you carry?" Char asked.

"It's a laptop, I use it to write my own stories. I've never had anything published, but I would like to. That's why I came here, to get inspired to start writing. Next time I come I will bring the laptop with me and show you what it can do. It's unbelievable to see the information that is available from all over the world, right at your fingertips."

Just then Rosie showed up.

"Rosie, I'm so glad you came! Lilly, can you see Rosie? Rosie is here with us," said Char. Lilly stood up, squinting her eyes. Sure, enough Rosie in all her glory had shown up.

"Hello, Rosie nice to meet you, I think."

Rosie said, "hello," with her hands on her hips as if to say, "What do you want from us?" Lilly could tell from her stance that Rosie had something to say, so Lilly spoke first.

"Hey, I have no idea what is happening here," said Lilly. "I am just as stunned as you are. Frankly, I was not sure if I would see anything the second time around. I thought maybe the other day I had a bit too much sun."

Lilly's arms were flailing about as if to say she still didn't understand what was happening. "For all I know someone could be watching and I'll be checked into a nut house any minute."

Rosie said, "That's a bit dramatic, isn't it?"

Lilly raised her eyebrows. "Well, maybe for you this is normal. I guess I should not be surprised; my whole life has been filled with weird shit! Hey, maybe this is another one of God's ways of using me for entertainment. Yeah, my life has been one chapter after another of pure amusement!" Lilly stood there with two spirits.

Charlotte and Rosie were already resigned to the fact that they were currently living sort of a shit chapter of their own.

Lilly started laughing at what she'd just said in front of these two women. Char and Rosie began to laugh and before long the three women were on their knees laughing.

"Ironic, huh?" said Lilly, "we are on our knees. Guess this is another side of God's humor."

The three women sat gazing out at the sea while the sun went down.

"Well, I'd better get going before they close the park and I get a ticket," said Lilly.

CHAPTER 14

Christmas bulb (kris'mes bulb): (noun) a holiday bulb hung at Christmas time, illuminates light with color.

Lilly parked the car near her hotel and decided to take a walk through town. She enjoyed the quaint shops and thought it could be fun to have her own shop. She considered what she might sell. She thought of a bookstore that also carried yarn, yarn you would want to run your fingers through. Yarn just felt yummy. Maybe some beautiful hand-painted dishes, with lavender and eucalyptus candles sounded so pleasant. She noticed a workman hanging some Christmas lights.

Instantly, she remembered years ago as a child she accepted a dare to steal a Christmas bulb off a neighbor's house. As she sat on the bench watching the man hang the lights, she remembered how mortified she was after stealing the Christmas bulb. She was shaken and thought someone would find out and she would spend the holidays in prison. An event she would never forget.

With a half-smile, Lilly wondered if she still had the bulb wrapped up in a box in the garage. She'd always thought she'd return the bulb during a midnight recon mission, no one would know. But as time went on, she figured she'd forgotten about the bulb.

Across the street Lilly noticed a plaque on a building. She walked over. It was oval, a dark color, with four bolts holding it. Established in 1800, it said. She wondered what this building was in 1800. She peeked into the window; looked like a general store with lots of character. As she entered the squeaky door a small bell rang to announce her entrance; she was instantly enchanted by the aroma of fresh bread.

"Ah, it smells heavenly in here," she said.

"Come in," said the clerk, "and enjoy a sample of bread fresh from the oven." Lilly's eye was caught by the super-size oven where obviously the bread was baking.

"Is this the original stove?" she asked.

"Yes, it sure is. The store started out as a general store and still is today." Intrigued by this information Lilly thought maybe she could learn some history while she sampled the bread. Hanging on the wall was a pair of old oars weathered by age. One oar had initials, carefully engraved.

"What can you tell me about the original owner of the store?" asked Lilly. The clerk looked about eighty years old; she wore a peach-colored apron over a long-sleeved flannel shirt, jeans, and glasses held by a chain around her neck. Her hair was short and sassy. You could tell by her energy she loved what she was doing.

She wiped her hands on her apron and said "Back in the late 1800s the store was owned by my great-great grandmother, Rosie Spencer.

Lilly was stunned, could it be the same Rosie she met at the Point? Her brain reeled, wondering how she could put all this together; she must plan another trip to the library soon.

"May I purchase a loaf of fresh bread from you?" Lilly asked.

"Of course, dear, what would you like?"

CHAPTER 15

Nurse [nurs]: (noun) a person trained to take care of the sick, injured, or aged.

"Here comes another spirit," Rosie said. "Let's go meet whoever it is." Rosie and Charlotte greeted this spirit like all the others, slowly and cautiously, never knowing how long it had been since they left their life.

"Hello," the woman said, "my name is Harriet." Harriet was a black woman she held her head high, hands folded in front of her waist, she had a scarf on her head. The scarf was tied tight, had white polka-dots, and lay flat and smooth, obviously done with care. She had a long black skirt sewn together in panels; her shawl was thin and frayed, her eyes were dark and steady. Char noticed that her cheekbones made her face look proud.

Harriet began to tell her story that she was born in Maryland, 1820 or 1821, she was not sure. She died March 10, 1913 at the age of 93.

"I died in New York of pneumonia," she said.

She told her story of becoming an African American humanitarian and Union spy during the American Civil War. She escaped from slavery and helped to rescue other slaves. She talked about how she was beaten and whipped by her masters. She explained her other name was "Moses" because she helped other slaves escape. She worked for the Union army as a cook, nurse and then as a spy. After the war she went home to Auburn, New York to care for her parents. The last thing she remembered was a bad case of pneumonia. After 93 years of life she was ready to go; she was worn plumb out.

Rosie and Charlotte were in awe of her story and all she had done; all she had endured. They felt small compared to Harriet.

"I heard Mother Theresa came through here. Did you see her, did you talk to her?" asked Harriet.

"No," they replied, "we have been here a long time and never have we seen the likes of her. Wait, a woman Teresa came by. But how did you know she was here?"

"Another spirit told me she came by Great Point where the lighthouse stands and that there were two women there reflecting kindness--you two." She pointed.

Again, Rosie and Char were perplexed. There must be a reason they were here; they just didn't know what it was. Harriet thanked them for their kindness and cup of tea. "I must be going; winds blowin changes are in the air."

Rosie nodded her head, "That's what we keep hearing, and I must say we have had some excitement lately."

Harriett walked down to the beach, picked up a stone and skipped it across the water with a smile on her face. She said, "I still got it." With a gust of wind, she was gone.

Charlotte looked at Rosie and said, "Where is that stash of Henry's wine you been hiding. I need a swig."

CHAPTER 16

Rip-tide [rip-tid]: (noun) a current opposing other currents, producing violently disturbed water, the strong, narrow flow of sea water that rushes seaward after incoming waves pile up on the shore.

Lilly decided to head back to the old library. She couldn't' wait to get back into the old books almost as much as she wanted to get back to Mr. Blum's coffee. Mr. Blum was there, as expected and so was the rich aroma of the coffee.

"Hello, Mr. Blum," said Lilly.

"Harry, please call me Harry."

"Okay, Harry, may I have a cup of that awesome coffee please?" No sooner had had Lilly finished her request than Harry handed her a steaming coffee mug.

"Where you starting to look today, Lilly?"

"Well, I already went through the section over there, to the left. I think I'll continue with the books right below those, if that's okay?"

Once again, she set up in the back corner so she could spread out. Lilly took a deep breath and rubbed her hands together as if she was preparing to throw dice.

A couple of sips of coffee and something caught her eye. The headline read "Fisherman Witnesses Large Funnel in

Water, Two Women Drowned." Could this be it? She leaned in and read on:

> *October 13, a fisherman known as Old Man Roberts witnessed a large hole open in the ocean. He described it as a funnel so deep you could look inside the belly of the sea. Old Sow, he called it. "I heard about these whirlpools but never seen one, he said. "I heard the rip is so strong, not even ten men could escape its pull, let alone two women." Roberts described how hard the women tried to row and push away from its strength. "I seen an oar ripped out of their hands like it was a toothpick," he said. He described how in an instant the women and the small boat disappeared. The boat was gone but the funnel kept churning, swallowing water like a thirsty whale. Charlotte Ridge and Rosie Spencer, deceased, drowned October 13, 1842.*

That was it, a small newspaper article described the last minutes of the two women who roam the Point. Lilly leaned back in her chair, trying to absorb what she just read, the brief but fatal struggle they endured.

"How's it going over here, Ms. Lilly?" Harry asked.

"Well, I think I just found the story I was looking for, but there is not much here. May I use the copier over there?"

Lilly decided to look further. Maybe services were held for Charlotte and Rosie. Maybe an obituary might give a bit more detail about these women. Another cup of coffee and Lilly settled into the old chair again. On the same page of the newspaper were the store hours of the Spencer General Store, the name of the latest ship getting ready to head to sea and the new location of the widow's walk which needed to be replaced due to the constant slap of ripples. In the next issue was a warning prohibiting swimming by the outlet or south cove due to the recent drownings due to the unexplained funnel. Town meeting tonight the paper announced.

"Town meeting," Lilly whispered. Were there records of town meetings stored somewhere? Obituaries...here was the one. She gently placed her finger along the words. Charlotte Ridge born 1796, died October 13, 1842. Wife of Henry Ridge, lighthouse keeper for approximately twenty-five years, additional family members unknown. Mrs. Ridge drowned with her longtime friend, Rosie Spencer, date of birth unknown, shopkeeper, bread maker, and family members also unknown. Drowning witnessed by fisherman Old Man Roberts off South Cove.

Lilly was interrupted by a sound. "Shush," said the woman who entered with two teenaged girls. The woman was tall and wore glasses and a t-shirt that said, "Peace Out." Shush again! The two girls were giggling and making snide comments about the library being "like really old and smelly."

"Where are the computers?" one asked. They continued to talk loudly into their cell phones. In contrast, the mother seemed just as intrigued with the place as Lilly was when she first walked in.

"You girls wait outside," she said, "I'll be right out." The few people in the library, including Lilly, were staring at her.

She said in low voice, "Sorry—the kids these days." This reminded Lilly of the episode she had seen on the ferry over, which brought a smirk to her face.

Harry approached. "What's so amusing that you have such a look on your face? Have you been able to find any more info on your story?"

"Yes, I have but I will need the next series that comes after this volume. I hope there is another volume?" she asked in anticipation.

CHAPTER 17

Sea breeze: a breeze blowing inland from the sea.

"One thing that seems to be routine for us is our teatime," Rosie announced.

"Yes, I so enjoy our teatime," said Charlotte.

"Sure wish that Lilly would come back to the Point since she is someone who can tell us a few things."

"Yes, I think she'll be back. Maybe she's going to bring us some knowledge of what happened to us. You nervous about that, Rosie?" Charlotte asked, as she poured the tea.

"What for, what can be worse than being already dead?"

"I don't know, just something about going back in time gives me the creeps."

Rosie started to laugh. "Woman, our so-called time is so messed up we don't know if we are coming or going."

Once again Rosie had a way of making Charlotte feel like everything was going to be okay, regardless.

"Now, let's just enjoy the beautiful sea breeze, Char. We gotta figure out a way to have cookies with our tea."

Lilly headed back to the lighthouse. She knew she'd been gone long enough and did not want her new friends to feel as if she was spooked off. She plunked down on her beach chair and waited for Char and Rosie to show up. It was not long before the hairs standing up on the back of her neck gave her the inkling they were close by.

"You're back," Char belted out.

"Good to see you again. You can still see us, right?"

With a smile on her face Lilly said, "Yep and I have some info about your deaths in the town's library. You still up for it?" she asked.

The three women sat on the beach and Lilly began to read the newspaper article, keeping hold of the paper so the wind would not rob them of their story.

"Sorry to say, not much here but I will keep looking. I rather enjoy the old library in town," Lilly said. She read out loud slowly and calmly, checking their faces to make sure they were willing to listen. Their fate, kept in an old book on the shelf, was now heard by their own ears.

"I read about these funnels before. They call them old sow because the noise it makes from the churning waters.

Charlotte's eyes began to well up. "I remember that sound like it was just yesterday. Remember Rosie? We didn't know where it was coming from. Old Man Roberts, remember him? He must have felt dreadful watching, unable to help."

"Read it again," Rosie said, "one more time please." Lilly gave them a few minutes, they looked out to sea as if they were replaying it in their minds.

"There's more," said Lilly.

"Rosie, the old general store is still in town. I think someone from your family works there, maybe a great, great, great, great, granddaughter. It's a beautiful gift shop. They also bake bread." Now Rosie's eyes were welling up.

Lilly continued, "The old bread stove is the original stove. That's what the woman told me. The smell draws you in. God, I love the smell of baking bread," Lilly said. "It's beautiful Rosie, I wish you could see it."

"I better go," said Lilly. "It will be dark soon. I'll be back tomorrow, ladies, will you be okay?"

Charlotte leaned in, "Thank you, Lilly, for doing this, for visiting us, and your box with the buttons. I hope we can do something for you someday."

Lilly was gone and the two women sat pondering what the day's events held.

"Well, we had some excitement today, huh, Char? I say we load up the tea pot." As they sat there, they heard a noise like scratching on the door. Just like every night the wind was blowing. As Rosie peeked through the door there was Pepper, the golden retriever they had seen days ago, only this time Pepper had a friend.

"Pepper, who you got with you?" Rosie checked the tags on the small dog, "Robie, his collar says." A beagle--both dogs were wagging their tails happily.

"I always wanted a beagle," Charlotte said, "Let them in. I believe this calls for two more teas." The two women and two dogs sat enjoying each other's company as if they were all old pals.

Lilly sat in her hotel room thinking about the day and what she would research next for her new friends. She figured she'd go back and visit the general store tomorrow.

CHAPTER 18

Carving [kar'vin]: (noun) the work of art of a person who carves, a carved figure or design.

It was overcast, gloomy, chilly–definitely a sweater day. She sure hoped that general store had decent coffee. She needed some. Lilly flung her knitted scarf around her neck and took a deep breath of cold air.

"God, I love it here--everything about this place," she whispered.

Lilly took the long way to the general store so she could see some of the local shops, particularly a yarn shop she noticed in the local paper named Liberty Ave Yarn. The window display at the yarn shop was carefully crafted of skeins of yarn shaped like a tree in colors of autumn. From the ceiling, icicle lights with knitted felted leaves, pinecones and acorns were meticulously placed, just beautiful. The window displays alone drew you in. As in many of the other shops, a squeak announced your entry. There was a candle burning, smelled like eucalyptus, earthy smelling. To the right was the sales counter surrounded by yarn, needles, buttons, books, and a pot of tea.

"Welcome," said the kind lady with white hair and glasses hanging around her neck; she could easily be pegged as a knitter.

"May I help you find anything?" she said.

"Oh, no thanks, I am just looking but I'm pretty sure I will find something in here that I must have," Lilly said with a smile. "Your display window is beautiful."

"Thank you, I was inspired by a large tree in my back yard. I get a lot of compliments on it, I must say."

"Well, it certainly drew me in," said Lilly.

It did not take long for Lilly to find several kinds of yarn she wanted; there was something about touching skeins of yarn that just felt yummy. Her creative juices were flowing; she thought she could sit in the shop for hours.

Even though she had a ton of needles, she spotted a set of hand carved #13 needles in the shape of trees and thought she must have these. Not sure if she would ever use them but it would remind me her of where she got them.

"Yes, these are popular, carved by a local wood carver," said the knitter.

An hour later Lilly was off to the general store. Warm bread always grabbed her like a snuggly sweater. She would have to get some bread to take back to her room or at least one of those large oatmeal cookies.

"Hello, I'll be right there, make yourself comfortable," yelled a voice from the back. This was Lilly's chance to investigate the oars hanging on the wall; she quickly pulled out her cell phone so she could take a picture of the initials carved in the wood. She needed to step up on a chair to look closer. The oars had a few old cobwebs; you could tell they'd been up on the wall for a long time.

"Admiring our oars, are you?" said the clerk.

"Oh, yes, I noticed there was something carved there and was just curious. It's a very old oar, huh?"

"Yes, back in the day you could see it clearly: "H & C."

"H & C. Do you know whose name these initials stand for?" Lilly held her breath in anticipation.

"Two people: Henry and Charlotte, I have been told."

Lilly rubbed her hand along the oar as if it had a soul to which she was connecting. "Wow, what do you know about Charlotte and Henry?" Lilly asked.

"They were lighthouse keepers. Henry was also a fisherman; all I know is the sea took him. Well, the sea took both. Charlotte was killed in a boating accident," said the clerk.

"So, what does this oar have to do with Charlotte and Henry?" asked Lilly.

"Geez, I feel like Inspector Gadget, any minute something stupid is going to spring out of my mouth."

Just then someone entered the shop.

"Good afternoon," said a gentleman with a cane.

"I need the usual dozen oatmeal cookies please," he announced.

Dang it, Lilly hoped he'd leave her a few cookies.

"Coming right up," said the clerk.

"Hey, Joe, this young lady is interested in the old oars."

He glanced up at the oars as if he had hung them himself.

"I was just asking," Lilly said, as she glanced over at the clerk.

"Rose is my name, but friends call me Rosie," said the clerk.

Good grief, Lilly thought the clerk was somehow joking.

"Rosie, hello, my name is Lilly and actually I'm writing a story about the two women who were swept up in a sow in the ocean. They were Charlotte and Rosie, so you can only imagine my astonishment as I stand here in your shop."

"My name is Joe," the old man said, "and Rosie here is my favorite sister."

"Your only sister," she yelled across the room.

Joe was of average height; his dark tan skin matched his dark hair. He wore a fisherman's cap, and a scarf that looked like it was bought twenty years ago. His fingers were bent and old. He had an old cane he used to maneuver about. Lilly noticed the cane had notches carved like a wave pattern. He certainly did not seem to need the cane.

"Can I get you two some coffee?" asked Rosie.

Joe answered for the both of them, "Yes."

"Oh, and a few of those oatmeal cookies too please," said Lilly. Joe used his cane to point to a table and chair in the corner.

"Sit down, young lady, and maybe I can help you with your story."

CHAPTER 19

Stranger [stran'jer]: (noun) a person not known or familiar to one person; is not an acquaintance.

Charlotte and Rosie were once again looking out to sea, waiting to see if any spirits would show up. Soon a man came walking down the beach, sizing up the lighthouse. The women watched as he strode by. Curious, Charlotte and Rosie followed him. They watched as he tried to open the lighthouse door. He looked around, making sure no one was watching. He pulled out a small packet of tools and proceeded to pick the lock. It didn't take long before he was in and quickly closed the door behind him. Char and Rosie jumped up like schoolgirls.

"This could be fun," Rosie said.

Inside the lighthouse you could hear the wind blowing. An orchestra of sounds over and over, never sounding the same. He held the railing and started the circle of steep stairs upward. He kept looking behind to see if anyone was there, readjusting the small pistol stuck in the back of his pants.

"Not a very big gun," Charlotte said.

Rosie had seen pistols and knew even the small ones could kill. Her uncle had visited; he carried a decorated pistol. He would tell stories of how he shot birds and other game to eat on his travels. His was made of polished wood and metal. Much bigger than what this man had.

Rosie thought it would be fun to see if she could touch his shoulder; would he get spooked out? Char's eyes grew big, with a cocked smile as if to say, I dare you. Rosie reached over and put her hand on his shoulder. Startled, he quickly whirled around. His chest was moving like a bellows as he started to move faster up the stairs. Finally, he stopped at one of the window port holes. The port hole was about three feet from the stairs, wide enough for a person to sit inside. The window was round, the view through the glass distorted by years of weather. The man once again pulled out his pouch of tools. He took a small knife and inserted it into the old bricks. Slowly, he pulled out three bricks. Charlotte and Rosie leaned, glancing at each other, watching what appeared to be a thief violating their home.

"What on earth is he doing?" said Rosie.

"Well, obviously he has got something in there."

Charlotte and Rosie waited in anticipation as he carefully pulled out a wooden box. The stranger took a deep breath and blew over it to remove the layers of dust. The box was brown with two hinges in the back and looked man-made. It had a brass bracket that circled it on each side with a brass latch held by two small screws.

"Well, well what do we have here?" Rosie whispered.

He then took his hand and ran it across the box. Slowly he opened it. The man exhaled in relief his eyes widening. Inside were coins, beautiful stones, and a few pieces of jewelry, but mostly coins. One coin fell to the ground. This gave the women a good look. It was mostly silver but had a gold cross. Each corner had a leaf-like shape and at the top was a design shaped like a draped curtain. Compared to the other coins, this one was small. Charlotte could see a sapphire ring held by a thin gold band. The stone was a beautiful blue color. It made her think of the deep sea.

The man whispered, “Still here after all this time; soon I will be rich.”

Quickly he closed the box and placed it back in the brick tomb, disguising it as if he had never been there. Just as quickly as he came in, he was out of the lighthouse. Rosie and Char followed him to make sure he was gone.

Just then, they noticed a spirit off in the distance. Roger was riding his lawn mower. Roger was a favorite of the women; he always had a way of making them laugh. Rosie had her hands on her hips with a grin on her face.

"Where does he get those shirts? I swear, they could part the sea," said Rosie.

Roger’s shirts were something right off Magnum PI. Bright colors, like he just left the beach in Hawaii.

“Hello ladies, just cutting the grass a bit and picking up some trash. Got to keep the place clean you know,” said Roger.

Roger was a handsome, friendly guy—the kind of guy who would give the shirt off his back if you asked. Although, no way would either Rosie or Charlotte be caught dead in that shirt.

“Hey, who was that guy?” Roger asked.

“Never seen him before,” Rosie said. I got bad vibes, especially when he flicked his cigarette at me. Course, I got him back cause in a few days he’s gonna wonder what that smell is in his car. Won’t take him long to figure out that it’s a dead fish!”

“Come on, Roger, have a cup of tea with us,” said Charlotte.

“Would love to, ladies, said Roger. “Hop on. I’ll try not to scare you to death,” he said with a laugh. “Did I ever tell you about the time I cooked a whole turkey in a trash can?”

CHAPTER 20

Lottery [late r e]: (noun) a game of chance in which people buy numbered tickets, and prizes are given to those whose numbers are drawn by lot: sometimes sponsored by the state.

Lilly walked as fast as she could down the beach. Each time she wondered if her new friends would still show up. A sigh of relief once she saw two faint dresses flapping in the wind.

Rosie said, "that sand sometimes feels like lead trying to get across it at a fast pace, huh?"

"No way, not to me," Lilly said. "Anytime I can get my feet in the sand is pure joy, I love it."

"Well, how ya been?" asked Rosie.

"I have a lot to share with you guys, I've been doing some homework," replied Lilly.

"Well, we have had a few adventures ourselves here, but you first Lilly," said Rosie.

The three women sat in the small inlet.

"I went back to the general store in town," said Lilly. "I walk in and notice a pair of oars hanging on the wall. I decide to stand on a chair and take a closer look. There are initials carved in one of the oars."

Charlotte now had her hands over her face and tears were welling up. She leaned forward.

"It's my oar, Henry's oar, with our initials," said Charlotte.

"I think it is," Lilly said. "But that's not all. I met the owners of the general store--Joe and Rosie are their names. They are brother and sister. Rosie is named after you," Lilly pointed out. "They are your relatives. So, I'm sitting there, and I'm thinking holy shit; is this really happening? Meanwhile, I'm trying not to blurt out, 'Oh, hey, I know the woman you're named after. She hangs out with another spirit at the old lighthouse and drinks tea'." Lilly did the old gangster nod of the neck and snapped her fingers.

Now, the three women were laughing in amazement, as if they'd known each other for years.

"Oh, I'm not done yet. In the general store there's a framed picture of a small boat," said Lilly.

Charlotte and Rosie looked at each other.

"Can you see the name of the small boat in the picture?" asked Rosie.

"Yep," Lilly announced.

"Well," Rosie blurted out, "what is it?"

"It's pretty worn, but you can see a few letters. The owners told me her name was Charlotte Rose. Let me guess," Lilly said. "Charlotte Rose was your boat; is this the boat you drowned in?"

Charlotte and Rosie sat in awe shaking their heads yes.

"So where is the boat now?" they asked.

"Would you believe, the Charlotte Rose washed up on shore in Spain? It is now a souvenir owned by the Spanish government. I remember hearing this story on the news. They tracked it down because of the registration numbers and knew its original home was in Nantucket," Lilly said.

"Here, I found a picture online." Lilly began to unfold the paper she had printed out like a photograph of an old friend.

"That's her alright, Char, we sure had some good times in that boat. She looks pretty beaten down," said Rosie.

Charlotte moved her fingers across the picture as if she could feel its soul.

"Well, girls, how do we get the two of you into town?" asked Lilly.

"We could use a change in scenery," Rosie said.

"Yeah, but how?" asked Char.

"Leave that up to me," Rosie said. Charlotte looked at her as if Rosie was keeping a long-lost secret.

"Pretty soon I will have to head back home, girls. My time here is getting short," Lilly said. "I wish there was a way I could afford to live here in town. I'm really gonna miss you guys. Any chance you could hook me up with the winning lottery numbers?" Lilly said with a grin.

Lilly noticed a look on Rosie and Charlotte's face, like two kids planning to rob a bank.

"Oh, my God, girls don't do anything crazy, okay?" said Lilly.

"Wait," said Charlotte, "what's a lottery?"

Soon someone came walking down the beach. Lilly, of course, had to look as if she was just hanging out by herself.

"Hello." It was the Harry from the library with his wife.

"Lilly, right?" he asked.

"Yes, hello, how are you? Well, I've missed your visits to the library and I was telling my wife your story," he said.

"Hello, nice to meet you," they both said at the same time.

"I was telling Maggie about your research and we decided to take a walk down to the Point. I had forgotten how beautiful it is here," he said. "The lighthouse looks as solid as ever, although the land has receded a bit over the years." Harry pointed out.

"Have you lived here long?" Lilly asked.

"All my life," Harry said, "and so has Maggie."

"Well, we won't keep you from your research," Harry said.

"Oh, Maggie, thanks for the pumpkin cookies; they were fabulous," said Lilly.

"Well, why don't you join us for dinner tomorrow night, I will make you a few more," said Maggie.

"Stop by the library at five p.m. and we can walk to the house together, its close by," Harry said.

"I will," said Lilly. "Should I bring anything?"

"No need to bring anything, but we would love to hear about your story," said Harry. And with that, Harry and Maggie continued their walk down the beach.

CHAPTER 21

Sand dollar: a round, disklike echinoid echinoderms that live on sandy ocean beds.

Lilly had a morning ritual, open the window at the hotel, stick her head out, and close her eyes.

"Ah fresh ocean air, I could never tire of that smell. Feels like another chilly day," she said. With her favorite sweater, she was ready to head out to the general store for a cup of coffee and an oatmeal cookie. Taking the long way, so she could absorb another part of town not visited yet, Lilly opened the general shop door. This time, feeling like she walked through a time zone--Captain Spock should be there to greet her.

"Good morning, Rosie, how are you?" asked Lilly.

"Good, what can I get you this brisk morning," said Rosie

"Hazelnut coffee and an oatmeal cookie—no, two please," Lilly said, pressing her lips together. Lilly sat in the corner, conjuring up how she was going to ask Rosie to visit the lighthouse.

"Rosie, you ever visit the lighthouse at Great Point," asked Lilly.

"Oh honey, I have not been there in ages."

"It's beautiful and I would love some company. Would you like to go with me today?" asked Lilly.

Rosie wiped her hands on the worn apron.

"I would like that, let me see if my brother will keep shop for a few hours.

Lilly, a little stunned, smiled. Well, that was easier than she thought.

Joe arrived with his cane, bopping around like a school kid.

"Finally, I get to spend a few hours behind the counter doing things my way," he said as he waggled his cane at Rosie.

"Funny Joe, real funny. Just don't leave me a big mess to clean up, would ya?" Rosie said.

"Yeah, yeah, you women get out and let me do my thing," said Joe.

Rosie turned around to Joe, "We have not had any of your Italian bread lately."

"I was thinking the same thing on my way over here," Joe replied.

Lilly drove down the windy road thick with trees, her mind racing. Would this Rosie know who Rosie was? Would the two be able to see each other? Either way she was doing the right thing. She just knew it.

"Lilly, have you heard there is a hurricane coming in a few days?" Rosie pointed out. Lilly snapped back into reality

"What? A hurricane, when?" Lilly asked.

"Tuesday, I think. You never really know how these storms pan out and the newscasts usually make it sound worse than it really is," said Rosie.

Lilly said "I haven't watched any TV since I've been here, just enjoying myself."

Rosie smiled at her. "That's good, Lilly. You're not missing anything."

Lilly pulled into the shell crusted parking lot.

"Here we are," Lilly announced.

"Let me get the beach chairs out of the trunk so we can sit and enjoy," said Lilly. The two women flipped off their sandals, both giggling once their feet dug into the sand.

Charlotte could see two women walking down the beach. It took her a few minutes to figure out who was coming. Charlotte raised her hand to her face to pull back the black hair covering her eyes. Soon, Lilly could see Charlotte in the distance, her dress blowing in the wind like a wild sail.

"Almost there," said Lilly. "I have a favorite spot in between the dunes where it's a bit protected by the wind. I have my hair to think about, you know." Both women laughed. "As any beach-dweller knows, you're going to leave with a different hair-do for sure."

"Here it is Rosie, right here, let me get the chair set up for you so you can be comfortable," said Lilly.

Lilly helped Rosie settle in, unwrapping the blanket so they could share in its warmth. "This is lovely," said Rosie. "Thank you for bringing me here. The lighthouse looks as sturdy as I remember."

Lilly, watched as Charlotte knelt down next to Rosie's chair. Charlotte knew who this was.

She whispered, "Her eyes are the same as Rosie's." She reached out to touch the top of her hand that lay on the arm of the chair. Rosie reached over and rubbed her hand as if she had an itch.

"It's just beautiful here, Lilly," commented Rosie.

"You will have to come and visit more often now that you know the perfect spot," said Lilly. Rosie looked at her and smiled.

Charlotte kept looking over at the lighthouse, wondering what was taking Rosie so long. Where was she?

Charlotte finally said aloud. "Rosie, I need you." Within a few minutes, Rosie appeared. "You okay, Char?" she asked.

"I'm fine, Rosie. I just did not want you to miss seeing family from the bread shop."

Lilly asked Rosie questions about the bread shop. Questions she thought Rosie might herself ask if she could. Rosie and Charlotte sat there listening, like two kids seeing a picture show for the first time. Rosie was in awe and touched Rosie a few times in an effort for some kind of family life connection. Tears welled up a few times.

"Look Char," Rosie pointed out, "she has flour under her fingernails just like I usta, remember?"

"Yes, I remember, can't you just smell the hot bread?" Char held her hands together as if she was holding a loaf to her nose to get the warm whiff.

"Lilly, it's so peaceful here and kinda strange at the same time," said Rosie.

"What do you mean?" Lilly asked.

"It's nothing, it's silly," said Rosie.

"What is it?"

"I almost feel like we're being watched, but safe at the same time," said Rosie.

"I feel the same way, Rosie."

Rosie looked over toward the lighthouse for a moment and then she noticed a sand dollar placed gracefully on the arm of her beach chair. Rosie gasped, smiled, and then slipped it into her pocket.

"Rosie, guess we better head back to the car before we get a parking ticket," said Lilly.

Rosie said, "Let's walk back...but slowly."

CHAPTER 22

Widow's walk: along the coast, a platform with a rail around it for observing ships at sea.

Lilly walked over to the library a little early. She wanted to look up a few things before her invited dinner. Just like before, the smell of the library hit her like a field trip to the museum. A few whispers, the squeaky floor, smell of Murphy's oil and stale coffee. Lilly gave a wave to Harry just to let him know she was there. She pointed to the back of the library. Harry was busy helping a few students from the local university who appeared to be working on a college project.

Lilly wanted to see if she could find a picture of the old lighthouse and its surroundings. Remembering what Harry had said about the earth receding a bit each year, she also was interested in the ships that came and went from the harbor. Maybe there was information on Henry and what his role was on the ship. The old widow's walk--if those wood planks could talk. The time she spent in the library seemed to fly by.

"You ready, Lilly?" Harry asked.

"Oh yes, sorry I lost track of time. Can I make a few copies quickly before we leave?" Lilly asked.

"Of course, no charge," Harry said with a wink of his eye.

"I'll turn off a few lights and lock a few things while you finish up," said Harry.

Soon they were making their way to Harry's house down Randal Ave.

"You really do have a short commute, don't you?" Lilly asked with a smile.

"I love my job," Harry said. "The short walk makes it even better. I get my exercise and I can go home and have lunch with Maggie every day if I like."

Their house was small, had a beautiful porch, a typical harbor home. Windows long, with views that included the town and the harbor. Shutter dogs graced the window shutters, twisted iron used to protect the windows for what was about to come.

"Wow, look at all those boats, what a beautiful view." Lilly said.

The house was warm and inviting. Lilly noticed a basket full of yarn and two large needles in the midst of a knitting project.

"You knit, Maggie?" asked Lilly.

"I love to knit myself," said Lilly. The two women started a conversation about the knitting store a few streets over. Lilly told her of the needles she purchased, and how they have trees carved on them.

Harry piped in. "Oh, she knows the store, too. Well, shoot I think she might as well set up a four poster bed over there."

Their kitchen was a good size with a large, beautiful marble island. Clean, white tiles encased the room. The flour and sugar jars looked as if they were handed down from generations. The best part of the kitchen was the brick fireplace.

"Oh, I always wanted a fireplace in the kitchen, it's wonderful," Lilly said.

"The gas stove is the other man in my life," Maggie said. "I love this gas stove." She ran her hand across as if to caress it.

Harry smiled and said, "And I'm okay playing second fiddle to the stove."

'I'll let you girls talk while I get a few things done before the great tempest hits," Harry said.

"I hope it's not a bad one this time," said Maggie. "I'm already tired thinking about a sleepless night." Soon dinner was over, and the wine glasses were empty. They all leaned back in their chairs in gratification for the meal.

"Oh my God, that was awesome; thank you for having me," said Lilly.

Lilly was envious of the relationship Harry and Maggie had. She wondered if they knew how lucky they were to have each other.

CHAPTER 23

Text: (text-ed) to send a typed message by cell phone.

Lilly started to think back to the last time she had a date. She met Don at a small reunion. A group of friends getting together for pizza on a Sunday afternoon. Don had no idea who Lilly was in high school. Their paths probably didn't cross except for maybe in the busy hallway. Don sat next to Lilly and had his arm resting casually on the back of her chair—an odd closeness. After a few hours they all hugged and said their goodbyes.

Within an hour, Lilly received a text message from Don, "Call me sometime, would love to go out, here is my number."

Flattered, Lilly sent a message back and said, "Let's meet for coffee."

A week later Lilly walked to the post office and then to Starbucks with a newspaper. She wanted to sit outside on the beautiful sunny day and catch up on the latest sports page. Don was charming and the conversation was enjoyable. At one point he had donut crumbs stuck on the side of his mouth. Guess she could have said "got a little something here" and pointed to the side of her own mouth. For some reason she decided to flick it off with a little grin. Occasionally, he would tell her how cute she was and reach out to hold her hand. A bold move for someone he just met.

After the visit at Starbucks, there would be phone calls, texts exchanged and the continual flirtation from Don. Careful Lilly: this guy is a bit too full of himself. You don't want to be reeled in by his charm. For some reason, still unclear to Lilly, Don would ask her out, make plans and then bail, float some excuse why he could not make it. His text would read, "Played golf and really tired, can we reschedule?" This happened three times. Again, the reply was "Can't wait to see you," and asked if he could call her that night. The phone conversation consisted of the day's events, no mention of him cancelling the date. Once again, a third date was planned, a movie and coffee. Forty-five minutes before Lilly was to meet him at the theater again, a text: "Too tired."

Ok, this guy is a jerk; I'm done, she decided. A week later, Lilly just happened to mention Don and the events that had occurred to Karen, another high school friend who was also at the same lunch reunion. The two gals were communicating via Facebook. It wasn't long before a reply buzzed from Karen, "He's a jerk, a dick," the message began. Karen had spent an evening with Don and was fooled by his charm. She went on with some of the same events, the same lame excuses. Both women used and manipulated. An odd abnormal feeling came over Lilly like the Grinch standing above a mountain top, an epiphany slammed against her chest. An instant wave of relief came over her. This one goes down in the books as the date that never was. Lesson learned, check. Due to the encouragement of friends, Lilly did the on-line dating thing. Dating, Lilly decided, is a way to figure out a person's true character–strengths and weaknesses.

CHAPTER 24

Harbor log (harbor-log): Nautical, that part of the log-book which belongs to the period during which a ship is in port.

"Now, tell us about the story you are writing," Harry asked.

Lilly proceeded to tell what information she found in the library about two women who drowned off the Point.

Harry stood and said, "I have something to show you. I'm not sure if this will interest you but I have a harbor logbook. This is from the harbor master, around the same time."

Soon Harry came back with a leather-bound book. It looked like something you'd see in a library at Hogwarts. Pages musty, tainted brown over the years. They made a crinkly sound as Harry opened the book as if the logbook gasped for air.

Lilly once again was in awe at what was within her reach. She couldn't help but think something or someone really wanted her to write this book.

"I gotta get my old lady glasses, so I don't miss anything," Lilly said as she reached into her purse. The pages were labeled at the top with dates, ships' names, cargo, crew names and a few other miscellaneous items.

Where did you get this book?" she asked.

"My grandfather had it, but I don't know how he came about having possession of it," said Harry. "I was always intrigued with it as a kid. He gave it to me after I finished school."

"Would you let me borrow it for a few days?" asked Lilly.

"Sure," Harry said.

"Glad that I can share it with someone. If it helps your book, I know my grandfather would love that."

"I will take good care of it, I promise," said Lilly.

Lilly gave her delighted thanks for the wonderful dinner. Harry insisted he walk Lilly back to the hotel.

"Now I insist you batten down with us for the hurricane," Harry said.

"Oh, yes thank you, Harry, good idea. Funny, I hadn't even thought about it. Yes, thank you. I really don't want to be alone when it hits," said Lilly.

Lilly went up to her room. She couldn't wait to get into the book. Quickly, she got out her notebook and pen, turned on the computer and started scanning the pages for the Anibell. She believed this was what Charlotte called the ship Henry was on. Lilly carefully turned the pages. Holding the logbook, she breathed in the smell. Her finger scrolled down the page looking for anything that might grab her.

"Anibell, Anibell, where are you?" she said aloud. The names of the crew, their dates of birth–some were just kids. On the right side of the page at the top just SOS "save our souls" in other words DOD "date of death." Some of the pages had no date in the SOS column, which meant their journey on the ships lasted for years. Occasionally a note referencing cargo.

1. *Fruit*
2. *Seeds, dirt samples*

3. *Stowaway*
4. *Gin and miscellaneous alcohol*
5. *Whale oil $$*
6. *Miscellaneous treasure, rhinestones, jewels*

Two hours and two glasses of wine later, there it was: Anibell caught in a storm. Making out the date on the top of the page. Approximately thirty-five crew members.

CHAPTER 25

Stairwell (stair-well) noun: a vertical shaft in a building containing a staircase.

Charlotte and Rosie enjoyed their visits from the dog spirits. Today, Robie and Pepper came running up the beach, like a whirlwind, chasing two cats in pure joy.

Rosie laughed. "Poor cats, they ain't got a chance with those two."

"That's it, Char," said Rosie. When I come back reincarnated, I wanna be a dog, a dog with big ears and big feet."

Charlotte said, "You gotta finish dying first, girl."

"Well, while we're waiting let's have tea," said Rosie.

As usual, tea was laid out in a prim manner. Only this time there was a bottle of ale. The dogs were curled up in the corner exhausted from their scuttle on the beach.

"They look so peaceful, don't they?" said Char.

Both women looked up and leaned toward the window.

"Hurricane not far off," said Rosie.

"What should we call this one?" Charlotte asked.

"Guess we should wait till it rolls in, get a feel for it," said Rosie. Even the dogs adjusted to a spot under the temporary tea table to take cover.

Rosie and Charlotte decided this was their chance to use the storm as an opportunity for Lilly to get rich off of the secret box hidden in the stairwell. A way for Lilly to move to the harbor and be close to them for however long they would be there. A way for Lilly to have her dream come true, a home by the ocean, get her book published.

It took a lot of concentration for the girls to move an item of that size and weight. They would have to make the stairwell look a bit damaged, but not too much. They had too much respect for the old lighthouse they called home. Hours went by as Rosie and Char bounced ideas around regarding what to do with the treasure in the box. Outside the wind was beginning to kick up. Every now and then a gust would hit the glass window. The atmosphere just added to the plotting going on.

CHAPTER 26

Hurricane (hur' kan): noun a violent tropical cyclone with winds moving at 73 or more miles per hour, often accompanied by torrential rains.

Lilly went down to the front hotel desk with a small bag. Important items she would need to ride out the storm with the Blums. She let them know where she'd be staying and that she would be back once the storm passed.

"Good idea," the clerk announced. "The Blums are good people, and you will be inland a bit, away from the harbor. Don't worry, your other belongings will be safe in your room." Just then the facility worker came by.

"Hey Lilly, you going inland a bit?" he asked. "I was just getting ready to finish up hanging the shutters over the windows, guess I can start with your room."

Lilly took a deep breath. "You guys be safe, and I'll see you in a day or so," she said.

Lilly walked slowly to the Blum's house. Everyone was out boarding up windows in an efficient manner. Obviously, they had done this many times before.

Lilly hoped the yarn shop would fare well. She peered through the crack in the plywood and could see crates of yarn all stacked methodically on a makeshift shelf off the ground. Plastic bins were full, attached with bungee cords hooked to the wall. Huh, she hadn't even noticed those hooks, pretty ingenious.

The bread shop was closed tight already. By now, wind was picking up and it started to sprinkle a bit. Lilly had decided to bring a bottle of wine she purchased at the beginning of her trip, along with a loaf of bread she purchased the day before. Harry was gathering up flowerpots in a wagon and putting them into the garage.

"Oh, let me drop off my stuff, I can help you," Lilly said.

"Sounds good, that would be nice," said Harry.

"I'll get you some gloves." Eventually, Harry and Lilly made it inside and closed the door. Harry bolted it as if we were keeping out the nightwalkers. The sound alone seemed so final. The three of them sat at the large wooden table made from old barn wood. Three glasses of wine and several candles were ready for what could be a long night.

"Well," Maggie said, "bring on the dominoes championship."

Lilly thought for a moment how Rosie and Charlotte would do in the old lighthouse with a storm slamming up against them. She soon decided they'd probably seen many storms over the years. What's the worst that could happen?

"You think the lighthouse will take a beating tonight?" Lilly asked.

"Yep," said Harry, but she has strong bones and a good soul. She has been through many storms, and this won't be the last."

"I've been going to the Point every day; guess I'm a bit worried if it will leave any scars," Lilly said.

"Oh, the sea will change it for sure...always does. Leaves a mark, like a good hard slap on the back," said Harry.

Just then the power went out.

"Here we go," Maggie said with a deep sigh. "Let's fire up the candles."

Lilly had told the Blums of how her mother had used solar lights from the garden in the hallway to guide her to the bathroom the last time they prepped for a storm. Kind of looked like a mini-runway. Worked great and they appreciated the idea. Hours went by while the wind unleashed its steady shrieks. A constant hum with the occasional wallop, a symphony so to speak. Lilly, Maggie, and Harry enjoyed each other's company, drank good wine, and ate a smorgasbord of food.

"I wonder how it's going out there; what will it look like in the morning?" said Lilly. The three of them decided to spend the night in the living room under blankets–Harry and Maggie on the couch and Lilly on the oversized leather chair.

At the Point, the hurricane slammed against the building. Wind swirling to and fro, back, and forth pulling up sand like a magic carpet.

Rosie glimpsed a familiar sight. "Charlotte, sea foam just like back in the day," she said.

Leaning against the window like kids watching it snow. Constant push of fluff, foam, and more sea foam. The color of a dirty t-shirt that has lost its pure white cotton color. Brown and green chunks of seaweed ripped from their foundation, dead algae. As Rosie and Charlotte watched the sea foam build, it felt like the lighthouse had left the planet. Maybe Poseidon himself would show up in all his majesty. Although both were intrigued by what was happening, they remembered the birds in the area had a hard time after the sea foam came and went. Once, they'd seen dead birds along the shore after sea foam heaved onto the beach.

Thoughts returned to the treasure. How were they going to convince Lilly to use the box in the wall to her advantage? Soon they had removed the box and returned the loose bricks like pieces in a large puzzle. The ocean outside was growing dark and restless. Waves were so big they seemed to move in slow motion before slamming themselves against each other.

Life below the sea was in turmoil; the usual hustle and bustle of inhabitants were absent. Tucked away in the abyss of hiding places deep down, shadows would appear and then shift again. The undercurrent was strong, mayhem if small fish were swirling in its grasp. The movement of a group of jelly fish was like an orchestration to a great symphony being played. Only the occasional large fish would venture up to take a peek but quickly turned around to find safety. Even the few sunken boats were used as shelter, shuddering back and forth even if it was just for a borrowed night.

The bow of a larger ship obviously struck something long ago, maybe another ship. Maybe a whale or maybe a massive wave, no one will ever know. This ship was broken in several places. Even though it was split, sea creatures had nurtured and accepted it like an old penny. Life had reformed and shaped it with waves of color that would change in the water's current. On the starboard side a name--time had worn its shape but not its identity, Anibell.

Outside of the Anibell lay pieces of furniture, broken bottles, dishes, and wood boards, not much else. A large old bell caught on a rope swayed with the current. Pieces began to shake loose. They began to float, on a mission, finally free from the old ship's grasp.

Charlotte and Rosie drank tea, as always, waiting for the night to pass, occasionally looking out the old house windows. They watched in awe when a snowy owl flew by. Pure white, like an angel. Its wings stretching wide, enjoying the ride of the wind. Its whiteness was only marked with two black spots. Something comforting about the owl fell across the women. They both sank back in their chairs, feeling the same comfort not saying a word. "Have we seen a spirited owl before?" asked Charlotte.

Curled up on the large sofa chair, Lilly woke up to the smell of fresh coffee under a homemade quilt, she couldn't have been more comfortable. As she sat up the Blums were in the kitchen making breakfast just like any other Sunday morning. "We still alive?" Lilly asked.

"We are," said Harry. "Want some fresh brew?"

"Yes, please," answered Lilly as she stumbled a little to the table.

"Still too dark out to see if it's safe," Harry said. "Don't want to go out until we know we're not walking into a land mine, you know. Never know what's on the ground."

Lilly agreed, as anxious as she was to see what damage had been done. She thought about Dorothy opening the front door at the Land of Oz for the first time.

After a perfect omelet and buckwheat pancakes, Harry unbolted the door. The sun was trying to find its way through the gray, heavy clouds. It was cold, damp and smelled like low tide had settled in for three weeks. Trees stripped, broken down, beaten by the night's wind. Roof shingles scattered about like a deck of cards. Neighbors began to trickle out waving as if to say, "We're okay too." The window shutters served their purpose. It was not long, and one could hear the echo of hammers prying them open.

Lilly and the Blums picked up the miscellaneous debris, helped neighbors, and replenished coffee pots almost like it was a neighborhood block party. Mrs. Blum wanted to walk down to the pier to see how the boats fared.

They walked in that direction. Most of the boats had been removed in preparation for the storm but a few had been beaten and tossed about. Some lying on their sides, a few just beaten and exhausted. They three stood there with coffee in hand in awe of what Mother Nature can pull off. She had slapped the earth hard and left a print.

"This place will be busy with workers soon, so we'd better check the bread shop and see when they'll be able to get to baking," said Harry. Lilly looked out toward the sea, her thoughts of the lighthouse weighing heavy on her mind. She bent down, picked up a shell, brushed it off and put it in her pocket.

The bread shop was fine. Boards were removed off the windows, the sidewalk swept, it couldn't be distinguished from any other day.

"What can I do to help?" Lilly asked. She was handed a cloth to clean off the dirty windows. Soon, the aroma of bread baking filled the air, along with the comforting smell of coffee. The locals were coming in for the occasional break –a meeting spot to check in on fellow neighbors. Slicing a piece of bread for a customer, Lilly noticed flour had oozed under her fingernails, and she felt a calming which put a smile on her face. It was at that moment Lilly decided she could love living in this community but how? How could she afford to move and find a new job? Lilly thanked the Blums for their kindness and comfort. Later, that afternoon Lilly eventually headed back to the hotel, planning her trip to the lighthouse for the next day.

Soon after dawn, Lilly jumped in the car, driving slow to the lighthouse, catching a glimpse of what the hurricane left in its wake. So sad to see old trees uprooted and pushed over. They were discarded like enormous toothpicks stripped bare by the harsh wind. Once again, she could see the tip of the lighthouse as she approached the parking lot. As she parked, she noticed the wooden sign with parking restrictions was on the ground in the distance, busted up.

"Hmm, view looks better without that stupid sign," she said out loud.

With her arms crossed across her chest holding her sweater closed, she headed toward the lighthouse, stopping to slip her shoes off. The beach grass looked a bit weathered as it waved hello. Lilly stretched out her hand while she walked by so the blades of grass could brush against her fingers. Looked like the Point held its own once again.

Lilly stood at the edge of the lighthouse looking up holding her hand above her eyes to block the sun–waiting, waiting to see if Charlotte and Rosie would show up.

"Hello Lilly," a whisper came. A faint outline of a woman appeared and then another.

"You guys okay?" Lilly asked. "I imagine you've seen many of these storms come through, huh?"

"Yes, and each time it's dreadful," Rosie said.

"It's taken us a long time to not be afraid when the wind comes," commented Charlotte. "You did okay?" Charlotte asked. "You were somewhere safe?"

"Yes, said Lilly. I went over to Harry and Maggie's house, the Blums, you know, the guy who works in the library? We drank wine, played dominos by candlelight. Have to admit, though, I was frightened at times."

"Lilly, we want to bring you into the lighthouse, to the

top. Will you come with us?" asked Charlotte.

"Of course, said Lilly, "but how will I get in?"

"We have our ways," said Rosie. "The door is open now; come in." The three ladies climbed the steps. Each putting their hands along the cold, twisted wall using it for balance. Lilly climbed each step wondering what it was like at the top. The air was cold and musty, a little like the smell of low tide. The faint sound of wind whistling, a steady hum could be heard. Every now and then Rosie and Charlotte turned around to see if Lilly was still there. Looks of reassurance were exchanged.

For some reason Lilly was thinking about the typical scene in a movie. There is a noise in the attic, dark music begins to play yet the main character heads up the winding staircase like an idiot anyway.

Finally, at the top, they entered a small room encased by large glass windows with a small table and two chairs. An old weathered tablecloth carefully placed on the round table enhanced by a tea pot and two cups. The tea pot was a sort of comfort to Lilly.

"Lilly, we want to give you something," said Rosie. "Something found in the lighthouse walls; we want you to have it. We were hoping you could do some exploring on that electric box you have, find out where it came from, who it might have belonged to."

Charlotte pointed to a small wooden cabinet with a wooden knob.

"In here is a box," said Charlotte.

Lilly bent down and opened the small door. She pulled out the old wooden box and placed in on the table. She looked the box over, and then peered at the two women as if asking permission to open it.

"Open it, child," Rosie said.

Lilly slowly lifted the lid being careful not to break anything. Charlotte suggested she take everything out so they could get a good look. Lilly gasped as she laid all the coins side by side, gazing at them closely.

"The dates are hard to read," said Lilly. "I can't believe how old these are and I can't even imagine the value."

"Look at the beautiful rings," said Charlotte. She reached down and picked up the blue sapphire ring, holding it between two fingers.

"It's just beautiful, Char," said Rosie.

Charlotte slipped it on her fragile finger and in that moment, she began to slowly disappear.

"Char, Charlotte," Rosie said reaching out for her. Lilly looked at Rosie and saw the sheer fright. Rosie glanced around the room. "Where is she? Where could she have gone?" said Rosie.

"What just happened?" said Lilly. Rosie sat down next to Lilly in wonderment. Lilly asked, "And about this box—is there anything else that gives a clue as to where it came from? Maybe Charlotte is there?"

The women carefully looked at the items. Lilly tried to find engravings on the jewelry, but the bands on the rings were thin, leaving little room for any kind of messages or initials to a loved one.

Lilly pulled out a notepad from her purse.

"I will take some notes, head over to the library with my laptop and see if I can find where this stuff may have come from," she said. She carefully drew an outline of a few of the coins and took notes as to what was on them. She drew sketches of leaves and crosses. Lilly even laid the paper on top of a coin, lightly rubbing the pencil to copy imprints of the coins. She pulled out her cell phone and took a few pictures.

"No one can know you have these items," Rosie said. "No one, not yet. We need to know if Char is safe."

"There's one more thing you should know." Rosie began to tell how they found the box. "It was a man in the lighthouse not long ago, before the hurricane hit. We watched him pull out some stones from the wall where this box was hidden.

I have a feeling he was a nasty character," Rosie said, "and I don't want you getting hurt."

"Charlotte and I can deal with him when he comes back," Rosie said with a grin.

"Show me where the box was hidden?" Lilly asked. Rosie led Lilly back down the twisted staircase. Once at the spot, Rosie pointed to the stones and said, "Here, pull this one." She pointed in the direction of the loose stones. Lilly began to pull out the stones, six of them. She laid them in order on the small window sill close by so she would know how to put them back. Lilly bent down to try and get a good look inside the small hole.

"It's dark in there," Lilly said. She pulled up her sleeve, put her arm in as far back as it would go, feeling the walls of the cold safe.

"There's something else in here," she pulled out her arm from the deep hole.

"A logbook, it looks like a ship's log book," said Lilly. She brushed the dust and dirt off the leather binder and began to untie the two strands of leather that kept its contents sealed.

"Wait, said Rosie, "let's put the stones back and head back up to the light in case Charlotte reappears." They closed up the hidden safe and headed back up the steps.

"You girls must have had killer thighs," Lilly said, "getting up and down these steps."

"Let's see what's inside that book," Rosie exclaimed. Lilly lifted the cover slowly, afraid the book might fall apart. It reminded her of the ancient books in the library. Old, musty, crunchy pages letting out a small scream from the adjustment. First page said, "Ship's Log" the next page "Identification" and below those words *The Anibell*. Rosie let out a small gasp and repeated the words slowly: "The Anibell".

"The Anibell is the ship Charlotte's husband, Henry, set out to sea on,"said Rosie. "The last time I saw the Anibell was many years ago, alive, from the dock."

CHAPTER 27

Sapphire (saf'ir) noun: a clear, deep-blue variety of corundum valued as a precious stone.

Charlotte was in a place she had never been before, nothing was familiar, but she was intrigued. An old stone house stood on a cliff. A different kind of breeze, the sea air was different.

"Where am I?" she whispered. The old stone house was big. It had lots of windows, overgrown tucked into a hillside ridge. The view of the sea was breathtaking. Off to the side of the house was a long stone wall about three feet high. It went as far as the eye could see, weaving in and out of the tall grass. Obviously, someone worked long and hard on this wall. As she got closer, she noticed pieces of paper rolled up, stuck in the small crevasses of stones—thousands of them, tenderly placed. She bent down to get a closer look.

"What does all this mean?" she whispered. Slowly she ran her hand along the wall, noticing other items...coins, beads, necklaces, pictures, bottles. "What is all this?" she said. Charlotte sat on the ground and decided to read one of the notes. She carefully removed a rolled-up note paying attention to where it came from, so she could put it back properly and unscathed. She unrolled the worn paper delicately.

Dearest James,

There is not a day that goes by where I don't think of you and wonder if you are alright. Not a day I ever forget to whisper out loud "I love you." I wonder if you are okay. I miss you. Please don't forget about me, please don't leave me. Love KK

"KK," she said. She rolled the note back up and placed it back in its resting place. Are all these notes to loved ones long gone? She looked at a few items--a small, pressed coin trimmed with gold; she flipped it over. "This coin is old," she said aloud. A white round button with a pin on the back, odd-looking. Lots of pennies and white stones placed in a stack. Small wooden boxes, sea shells resting on the man-made wall. Mostly though, lots and lots of rolled up notes. Charlotte felt uneasy reading them. As if she was going through someone's private belongings.

Charlotte noticed someone approaching on a bicycle further down the wall. She stood, wondering if this was a spirit." Char began to run in the direction the bike was coming from. Taking a chance she might be seen somehow. Maybe she could find out where she was. The strange woman got off the bike, stood there staring at the gravestone wall. She looked exhausted, her face tired, her hair windblown. Charlotte noticed she had a nice sweater, one like Lilly would wear with big buttons. Charlotte stood next to her. It did not take long for Charlotte to figure out she was undetected. The woman laid the bicycle on the ground, put her hand in her pocket and pulled out a note. She held it close to her chest, and closed her eyes for a moment. The note was lovingly rolled up. She bent down to examine the wall.

"This looks like an honorable spot," the woman said. She pulled out a stone, placed the rolled-up note inside the wall and put the stone back in its place. Charlotte could tell this woman was hurting. The woman's shoulders looked heavy with grief. Charlotte placed her hand on her shoulder. The woman got back on the bike. Before she headed off, she took notice of the beautiful view. Drawing a deep breath of sea air she left.

Charlotte looked back at the old house. "Where am I?" she said. Looking down at her hand she wondered if the ring she placed on her finger had something to do with her new location. She wondered if Rosie was worried; would she ever get back to the Point? Curious, she had to investigate the old house.

Charlotte could tell in the back of the house there used to be a garden. An old wooden fence ravaged by wind, lots of weeds, an old shovel and rake left behind. The rake's teeth were now molded, rusted into the earth. A few gravestones stood off in the distance covered in moss. This old house no longer had living occupants. Maybe there was a spirit here who could help figure out where she was.

Once inside, she noticed worn furniture beaten by the wind. What once were paned windows were shattered.

How many seasons had gone by? Torn wallpaper, broken glass. Yet some windows and doors were boarded up, supposedly to keep intruders out.

Charlotte noticed the railing along the stairs. Why was there no dust on the railing as on everything else in this old house? Was someone here? Charlotte looked up the stairwell for any signs, listening for noise. All she could see were beams of light coming through a hole in the ceiling.

She decided to head up the stairs, slowly peering through the sunbeams for any form of life. At the top of the stairs were a pile of books, ships' logs, history books. Newspapers yellowed over time, some carefully stacked. Some books had dust on them, others did not. Peculiar. She bent down to get a closer look. Charlotte headed further down the long hallway until she glimpsed a man sitting at a desk, his back to the door. He was engrossed in whatever he was reading. Charlotte had a feeling, a hunch this was a spirit like her. His boots were black and worn, boots like she remembered seeing on Main Street when she was alive. Suspenders strapped his shoulders. This was a fisherman, maybe from her time.

"Hello there," she said as she carefully entered the room. The man stood, a bit startled. He was a tall man with dark hair pulled back in a ponytail. Looking at Charlotte, his eyes squinted a bit as he reached for his spectacles. He drew closer to her, examining her face.

"Char, Charlotte, is it you?" he asked.

Charlotte stood for a moment. She drew her hands up to her face as tears began to well. "Henry," said Charlotte.

He lifted his hand to hers and then held her for a while. As he drew back, he noticed the sapphire ring.

"Where did you get this?" Henry asked.

Charlotte explained how she came across the ring in a small wooden box hidden in the wall and it was when she tried it on that she was brought here.

"That ring, I had it made for you. I was going to give it to you as a gift when I returned," he said.

"I carried it in my pocket for months and then, our ship was assaulted with the worst storm. I went down with that ring in a wooden box clutched to my chest," said Henry.

She whispered aloud, "Wooden box?"

"Did the wooden box also contain coins," she asked.

"Yes," he said looking perplexed, "how did you know? I found that box in a cave during our last landing."

Charlotte continued. "Did the wooden box have man-made hinges on the back and a latch?" "About this size," holding her hands about a foot apart.

"And a bit heavy," she said.

"I don't understand, how do you know this?" Henry asked.

Charlotte began to tell the story of the old lighthouse and the Point. How she and Rosie watched a man pull out bricks from the old lighthouse which hid a box and its contents, jewelry and some old coins.

Charlotte began to tell him about Lilly.

"Lilly is the only living person who has been able to actually see me and Rosie," said Charlotte.

"All the years we have been stuck at the lighthouse. Lilly shows up one day with a thing she calls a laptop. I call it a lap box. It has buttons with letters and when you press the buttons letters appear on this thing," she said in excitement.

"I punched in my name on the lap box thing, and we have been kindred spirits ever since. We can see each other. It's wonderful. I so look forward to her visits."

"This man who has hidden my box, who is he?" Henry asked.

"He is a thief for sure; that much we figured out." Charlotte sat back in the chair and folded her arms across her chest, "Yep, a sneak and a thief."

"Rosie and I have already taken the box out and hidden it somewhere else so he can't find it," said Charlotte.

"We were showing it to Lilly, so she could find out where the box might have come from. She can research stuff on her lap box, anything. I don't understand this lap thing–it has a mind of its own. She also reads books at the town library. It's still there, Henry, the old library." "It sounds amazing," said Henry.

"Anyway, we were showing Lilly the items in the box so she could help us. I put the ring on and next thing I know, here I am, outside by the old wall," she said.

"I have to get back, Henry. I can't leave Rosie alone and Lilly. Will you come with me and...?" Charlotte stood for a moment and stopped mid-sentence.

"Maybe it's unfair for me to ask you to come. I'm sorry, I have no idea what you have been through. Do you have a purpose here in this house?" asked Charlotte. "I don't even know if there is a way for you to come back with me honestly."

CHAPTER 28

Thief (thef) noun: a person who steals. Esp, secretly, one guilty of theft or larceny.

Lilly, went back to the library with her note pad and laptop eager to start her research. Funny how she kept getting pulled back to the old library.

"Good morning, Harry," she said. "I don't know anyone who can make coffee smell as good as you do."

"You onto another investigation today?" Harry asked.

"Yeah, sorta. You know making up stuff for a book. Gotta make it look like I have some of my facts straight." Lilly didn't want to share any of the details as Rosie suggested. After all, her friendships might be at stake here. Lucky for Lilly, the middle school kids were visiting and he had his hands full.

Harry made sure Lilly had her usual spot in the back corner where all the old books were—the same books he shared with her a few weeks ago. Lilly and the old books were like long lost pals now. She knew where to look, which ones coincided with the days when Charlotte and Rosie were part of the community. She found sketches of the old coins, coins from the 1800s and how they were first used instead of written bills. Coins made by craftsmen who used molds. There was a recent story on CNN of a coin that sold at an auction for over a million dollars. To Lilly, they appeared to be similar to the coins in the box.

"God, these women are rich in a warped kind of way, and they don't even know it," whispered Lilly.

After four hours and three cups of coffee, Lilly still could not find any trace of the rings she took pictures of. At the time there were few men who could make jewelry like what was in the box. Any jewel makers she'd read about seemed to live in remote areas such as islands that don't exist anymore. It did suggest that often remote areas were the ones where precious jewelry was found on treasure hunts. There had to be a connection with the Anibell. She put her hand to her chin. Maybe she'd better start looking in another direction.

"Anibell, Anibell," she whispered. Turning the pages she seemed to be waiting for something to just jump out. Ships port logs, she slid her index finger down the page along the names of the ships. "There's Anibell," Lilly said.

'Manor Island, 1800 something,' couldn't make it out. Anibell docked for three days. Lilly fired up her laptop and looked up Manor Island. Small port for ships to dock, sell and trade, residents approximately 100 to 150.

One tradesman, listed as a jewelry maker, precious stones, able to melt gold and silver set in handmade molds. Went on to say the island disappeared into the sea due to erosion and typhoon abuse. Treasure hunters were known to have found many items in the area. Lilly leaned back in her chair, rubbed her hands across her face and let out a deep breath. Packing up her belongings she headed back to the Point. She couldn't wait to share with Rosie what she found. Was Charlotte back at the Point yet? Had Rosie lost her friend forever?

Rosie was sitting outside looking across the vast sea, wondering where her friend had gone. Would she be back? "Am I alone now?" She let out a deep sigh.

Once again, a spirit approached Rosie, a small woman. She had grayish blond hair, was short and walked with a bit of a limp. She was wearing a house dress with large pockets and eyelet trim, blue and white with small daisies. Just like their tablecloth. Her face had a scar that circled her mouth, a burn scar. Nonetheless, the scar was graced with a beautiful, comforting smile.

"Hello," she said.

"Hello, my name is Rosie, and welcome to the Point."

"I'm Josephine, Josie for short."

"Do you know why I'm here?" Josie asked.

"Nope, spirits pass by all the time, and we have no idea why." Rosie explained how she and Charlotte seemed to be the only ones who stay here. Many others had stayed for just a bit, some had gone quickly and some returned with no explanation.

"I was just getting ready to make some tea. Would you like to join me?" Rosie asked.

"Yes, I would love some tea," said Josie. The two women climbed the stairs to the top. Josie took in the view for a few moments. They sat down while Josie asked a few questions.

"Do you know where other spirits have gone after they leave here?" Josie asked.

"I don't know," Rosie said. "Most we don't see again and those that do come back it's as if they never left or they don't remember ever being here." Rosie paused. "Charlotte and I stopped asking questions after a while. We just enjoyed the company. Some are still in pain from the whole death thing; others are glad to be free from where they came."

"Did you hear that?" Rosie asked. It sounded like the door below closed. They headed down the twisted stairs.

"It's him," Rosie whispered. "Well, this should be interesting..." Rosie gave Josephine the abbreviated version of the man and the box.

"A thief I'm sure, you up for some fun, Josie?" asked Rosie. "I really want to make sure this thief never comes back."

"Well, I have nowhere else to be," Josie replied.

The husky man had the gun stuck down in the back of his pants. He climbed the stairs to the spot where the box was once housed. He pulled out the bricks as before, only this time not caring how he might put them back. He threw them every which way like potatoes. He bent down and pulled a small flashlight out of his coat pocket. Feeling around, he anxiously began stretching his arm this way and that. He quickly realized the small tomb was empty. Snarling, he reached in again--desperately. Rosie gave Josie a nod. At that moment he heard a noise. He lifted his head to listen. The sound of a finger squeaking on the round glass window above his head. Josie was slowly writing the words "get out." Then Rosie flicked a stone which bounced off the back of his head and rolled down the lighthouse steps. The sound echoed as the stone bounced off the twisted walls. The man quickly turned around with horror on his face. Rosie flicked another stone that hit him smack in the center of his forehead.

"Who's there?" he yelled. Again, Josie ran her finger across the damp window. As he spied the words, his body began to shake. He pulled his gun and began shooting into the darkness. The man fumbled and almost fell trying to escape the lighthouse. He lost his footing. Unable to control his sheer bulk, tumbled down the narrow staircase smacking against the walls as if the lighthouse was punishing him. Finally his broken body rested at the bottom of the stairs. He lay still and lifeless, only his nerves causing an occasional twitch.

The two women stood there.

"Now what are we going to do?" Rosie said with her hands on her hips. Was he alive or dead? Would he end up as a visitor at the Point?

CHAPTER 29

Loco; slang for crazy.

Lilly stopped by the hotel and dropped off her laptop. She shoved her notepad in her large pocketbook. This time she grabbed her camera, making sure her beach chair was in the trunk of the car. The anticipation of the delicious salty ocean breeze was like that last bite of an ice cream cone.

Driving down Main Street she noticed a sign in a storefront window: Art show this weekend. "Huh," she murmured. "I will have to make sure I stop by and support the locals. She giggled. If the "locals" knew what she had seen in the last few weeks they would think she was loco.

Lilly parked the car, slipped on her flip flops, and grabbed her chair. Lilly noticed there was another car parked in the small lot. Who was on the beach or at the lighthouse?"

As Lilly walked down the breezy beach, she didn't see any other beach chair, no kids playing in the sand, no couples walking hand in hand. No sign of life. She approached the large lighthouse feeling welcome once again. Lilly opened her beach chair and sat down, letting out a deep sigh.

"I will never tire of this place," she said aloud. The breeze was warm and comforting. Sea birds were squawking–speaking to each other. It was not long before Rosie appeared looking a little flustered.

"Rosie," Lilly said, "any sign of Charlotte?"

"No Charlotte," Rosie replied as she wiped her hand across her forehead.

"Don't lose hope." You guys are kindred souls, I believe she'll be back," said Lilly.

Rosie sat down in the sand next to Lilly.

"Listen, we have another spirit here with us; her name is Josie. She recently left your world.

"Oh," Lilly said. Her eyes softened as she felt the grief. Lilly was looking around in the open air.

"Hello Josie, I am sorry for you, for your family. This beach, Rosie is a good pit stop for wherever you are heading." She gave her a gentle smile. Josie knelt in the sand and leaned in, squinting her eyes. Reaching out toward Lilly, she said, "I feel like I know this person but I can't remember."

CHAPTER 30

Leather Binder; a hard cover in which paper documents are carefully kept.

Henry began to tell his story.

"I've been here at this place ever since I can remember."

"I don't know why I'm here. Once I figured I was not going anywhere I decided to take care of the notes in the wall outside, comfort those who come and visit," he said.

"I really don't know if I am a comfort. No one has seen me but sometimes someone shows up and I know they can sense my presence."

"I think what happens is they think the person whom they are leaving the note for is there, but it's me. I go along with it.

"Sometimes I blow on their face, touch a cheek, flip the note. I kind of enjoy it; makes me feel like I'm still living," said Henry.

"I want to show you something," Henry said. He reached down to a drawer in a small wooden nightstand and pulled out an old leather binder. The binder was thick held closed by a piece of leather tied in a bow. Henry began to untie the knot and flipped open the binder. The old, yellow pages contained a list of all the notes stuck in the wall. Names, love notes, Dear John letters, loved ones lost at sea. Random stories to lost loved ones.

"You copied all the notes in the wall?" Charlotte asked. "This must have taken you a long time," she said.

"I had nothing else to do," said Henry.

"Once I started reading the notes it was like reading a novel, Henry said. "Each note was a new story. Some short, some several pages long. Every day I copy the new notes, new letters put in the wall."

He hesitated. "It took a long time but eventually I got caught up. Sometimes I would pull out a note, a letter I had already read amused at myself that I could remember. It started to feel like the people in the letters were family."

Henry stood at the window looking down on the wall.

"It's the one thing that gave me meaning," he said. Charlotte flipped through the pages. Each letter had a name. Some had dates. Some were drawings.

"There must be thousands here," she said.

"Over three thousand."

He reached over to Charlotte and held her close to his chest. He lifted his hands holding her cheeks and slowly kissed her. Tears were running down Charlotte's face, her heart pounding. Soon his embrace ran down the small of her back, holding her tight. Breathing heavy they soon found themselves on the floor. Henry's hand making its way up the thigh of her leg, caressing her breasts in his hand. Charlotte's back arched by the sheer touch of him.

Hours passed as they lay on the floor holding each other.

"Charlotte," Henry said.

"I have no problem leaving here to go with you to the Point," he said. Charlotte pulled Henry closer.

"Okay, how do we get back to there? Rosie must be going crazy with worry by now," said Charlotte.

The next day Charlotte woke up, still on the floor,

wondering where Henry had gone. Quickly, she discovered he was outside squatted by the wall writing something down. Next to him stood a man—average height, his hair color tinted with gray. It appeared he was preparing to slip a note into the sacred wall like many others before him. He stood for a while and then peered out at the ocean to comfort himself, maybe seeking to let go of the past. He bent down and slipped the note in. Moving down the beaten trail, he walked closer to the deep blue sea. It seemed to calm him. The wind was swirling around his body. Charlotte knew this gift the ocean granted. A simple endowment of comfort.

Henry had his leather binder and pencil, and he sat up against the wall jotting down a copy of the letter with compassion. The man sat at the end of the trail for about an hour, obviously sorting out his thoughts. Finally, he brushed himself off and headed out but not before plucking a few wildflowers and placing them on the wall.

Charlotte walked out cautiously, not to interrupt the man's visit—watchful, not sure if the living spirit might be able to see her.

"Good morning," Henry said.

"I have an idea about how we might get back to Rosie," Charlotte said. "Not sure if it will work but I guess it's worth a try," she said.

Back in the old house Henry grabbed a few items, placing them in a worn satchel made of old leather. Charlotte pulled Henry close to her, giving him a kiss. With her hands hugging his neck she whispered in his ear and slipped the blue sapphire ring on her finger.

CHAPTER 31

Dead (ded): adj: Naturally without life.

"Lilly, you need to get out of here right now. "There is something I need to take care of and you can't be here," said Rosie.

Lilly looked at her a bit perplexed.

"Just trust me; it's better if you are not here."

"Does this have to do with the car in the parking lot?" Lilly asked.

"Don't ask any questions just go, woman!" said Rosie.

"Okay Rosie, I will see you tomorrow, okay?" Lilly said.

"Yes, of course," Rosie said. "Come back tomorrow."

Lilly pulled out her cellphone and took a picture of the license plate in the parking lot curious of what was about to go down.

Back in the lighthouse, Rosie sighed,

"Now how to get rid of this thug?" The man was lying at the bottom of the cold steps, lifeless.

The sun was setting, dark clouds were rolling in on the back of harsh winds. Perfect setting for getting rid of a dead body. "Storm's coming," she whispered. Rosie, succeeded in getting the heavy body to a small shipwrecked boat tucked away in a nearby inlet. The boat was overgrown by small inhabitants; twisted seaweed managed to keep it connected by the nature-made pier. She dragged the corpse into the boat and dislodged the craft from the grasping weeds and vines. Then she stood on the rocks watching the sea suck the small boat out to sea, a sacrifice to the sea gods. The further it went out, the smaller the burden appeared until it was swallowed up.

The wind swooped up and around Rosie, lifting her hair, puffing her dress up. It was as if the universe cleansed her of what she had just done. Rosie was reminded of the little boat that sucked her and Char in like a giant's gulp. Seemed like a very long time ago.

Rosie made her way back to the lighthouse. She wondered how she was going to tell Charlotte of the events that occurred while she was gone. Rosie turned around looking out to sea, ensuring that the old boat was not coughed back up for some reason. Lifting her hand to her head, she pushed the hair out of her face.

"I need a cup of strong tea," she said.

Charlotte and Henry stood there holding each other, lifted their heads.

"Where are we?" Henry asked.

Charlotte opened her eyes slowly. She still had her arms around Henry's neck. There they stood incased in the dark, tight stairwell. Worn bricks and a small circular window.

"I know this place, the smell. Oh my God, we are in the stairwell of the lighthouse! "He said.

Charlotte bolted up the stairs like it was Christmas morning. She knew these stairs like the back of her hand. Pulling up her dress, she took three steps at a time. Henry, on the other hand, was feeling his way slowly with little moonlight.

The door bolted open with such force the daisy printed tablecloth flew up on one end. There sat Rosie.

"Well, I'll be," she said.

Charlotte ran to hug her.

"It's so good to see you, Rosie. I was so scared I would never be able to come back to you, to the lighthouse."

Rosie had a tear running down her cheek with a silly grin on her face. She lifted her hand to Charlotte's cheek. "I have so much to tell you."

"Where have you been?" asked Rosie. Just then Henry walked through the small doorway. It took Rosie a minute, squinting her eyes. Looking the man over from top to bottom.

"Henry, is that you?" Rosie asked.

"Yes ma'am, it's me." Dropping his leather satchel, he held out his hands to give Rosie a solid hug.

"The ring, Rosie, the ring--it took me to Henry. I'm sure of it," said Charlotte. "This ring." She held out her left hand to show Rosie.

"This was bought by Henry for me all those years ago," she said. Charlotte stood, tears welling up.

"He put it in a wooden box, our wooden box."

CHAPTER 32

Cane (kan) noun: walking stick used for support in walking.

Lilly was back in her room wondering what Rosie was up to. She decided to sit on the balcony for a while and do some reading. She sat there pondering what had happened to her over the past few weeks, how could she explain this to anyone? Would she even try? She decided to jot down a list, make some notes of how she met Rosie and Charlotte, the lighthouse, her trips to the old library, the hurricane, and the pair of oars hanging on the wall. The other people she met. At that moment she decided this would be her story, her book! Lilly had totally forgotten about the chief reason for her trip. To write a book and now she had her story; it would be fiction. Well sort of, but it would make a beautiful book.

Thunder was rolling off in the distance, clouds were slowly making their way closer with the occasional lightning strike, a slow rumble of thunder echoing for miles. Even the birds were making a commotion deciding where to take safe haven. Lilly decided to head back over to the library. Better take her umbrella. Lilly loaded up her laptop, notepad and headed down Main Street. She hoped the coffee pot was brewing over there. Lilly decided to take a quick stopover at the general store and see what was baking. The gentle sound of a small bell rang to announce her presence. The whiff of pumpkin bread drew her in. Her eyes quickly took in the oars still hanging on the wall.

"Hello there," said Joe. "Pull up a chair and sit a spell, young lady. How is your story coming along?" Joe popped up and poured Lilly a cup of coffee along with two of the largest pecan oatmeal cookies.

"My story is coming along," said Lilly. "Just getting started but I have a few good ideas."

"This place sure is inspirational, I just love the Point. On my way to the library for some more research. It's more fun digging through the old books," she said.

"Yes, the old books have a lot of history," said Joe. "Harry and his wife have taken good care of the place."

"Joe, would you like to take a ride with me to the Point?" Lilly asked.

"I could use some good insight, you know, history about the lighthouse for my book," said Lilly.

"I'd be glad to help you," Joe said. The next day Lilly picked up Joe.

"Let me grab my jacket and a few cookies," he said. "Cookies always taste better on the beach. That and a fine glass of wine." Joe grinned at her. Lilly was excited and anxious at the same time. What would Joe experience, if anything?

Once at the beach, Lilly parked the car in the usual spot under a shady tree. She grabbed a notebook, pen and the small bag that contained the precious cargo. Oatmeal cookies and two beach chairs. Lilly and Joe headed toward the lighthouse. Joe walked slowly using his cane, soaking in the surroundings. A slight smile lightened his face. He was enjoying this.

"I have not been here in months. The sand has shifted a bit," said Joe.

As they headed toward the lighthouse, Lilly wondered, would Rosie figure out Joe was family? Would Joe sense her presence, or better yet would he see her as she did? Joe stopped looking off in the distance at the open sea pointing his finger at a dark cloud that was hovering closer. It looked like it would bring thunder, along with a sheer grey curtain of pounding rain. To the left of the massive cloud was a waterspout moving up and down graciously swaying on the water gaining momentum, delighting in its own motion.

Lilly was mesmerized by its power and how beautifully it moved, like a dance. The two of them stood there watching it for about five minutes. The sky let go of it like a wet beach towel tossed aside. It was gone.

"That was amazing," Lilly said.

"I've seen a few in my day," Joe said, "but I must say that one was one of the largest I've seen."

Thunder rumbled off in the distance as they pressed on.

Once at the lighthouse, Lilly set up the chairs.

"This is my spot," Lilly explained. "Keeps me a bit out of the wind between this little cove and the lighthouse."

Joe slowly lowered his body, carefully positioning his cane in-between the chairs.

"Can I ask what the notches mean in your cane?" Lilly asked.

Joe looked at her with heavy eyes.

"Yes, each notch is for a friend I lost at sea," he answered. "I've had this cane for many years. One of the merchants in town lost a family member at sea and carved it for me after I wounded myself trying to escape a sinking vessel. I'm eighty-one now. I've seen a lot of tragedies and have been lucky enough to have fished with some great men. The sea has given to me and taken away--that is the way of things. Never take for granted what she can do." Joe was looking out upon the water, giving it a nod, a gesture of affirmation, an acceptance.

CHAPTER 33

Fisherman (fish'erman) noun: a person who fishes for sport or for a living.

Rosie noticed Lilly was back and she had company. Rosie, Char and Henry wandered over for a visit, curious about who the new visitor was. Lilly's heart started to pound, wondering if Joe would get a sense of the lighthouse inhabitants. Would he suspect the occupants?

"Charlotte is here. Thank God," Lilly whispered. She leaned back in her chair with relief as she let out a deep breath. Lilly wanted to ask a million questions but couldn't in front of Joe. He'd think she'd flipped out for sure.

Rosie, Charlotte, and Henry knelt down in front of the two chairs. Lilly smiled and waited a minute. Henry stood up, peering down the beach. "Someone else is coming," he said. About two dozen spirits were headed toward them. Henry asked, "Are they all spirits?"

"Looks that way," Rosie announced. They were all lovers of the sea, fishermen for sure. Henry could tell by their dark, wrinkled skin.

"Can they see us?" asked Henry.

"We will find out sure enough," Rosie said. Charlotte was watching Henry in his wonderment, excitement in his eyes. Where had they come from? Lilly was holding in her excitement even though she could not see them herself.

Joe's head turned, he squinted his eyes, leaning forward in his chair.

"You see that? What on earth?" said Joe.

A heavy, grayed haired old man knelt down in front of Joe slowly reaching out to touch his cane. "I know this man, I know this cane. Joe, you dead?" he asked.

"Holy shit, I think I'm losing it," Joe exclaimed as he rubbed his hands across his face.

"You see this, Lilly, you see this man in front of me, and you see all these men?"

Tears began to run down Lilly's face. A sigh of relief, finally, someone to share this with.

"No, but I do see three other people," she said.

"People I have seen since I showed up here. I too thought I was losing it. It is such a relief to share this with someone."

"You know these men?" she asked

"Yes," Joe said, "these are my comrades long gone, the notches on my cane."

"William, is that you?" Joe asked.

"Yes, old man," he said with a quiver in his voice.

"You have not been here in a while," Will said. He had a scar on his neck about four inches long. Like most of the spirits that come by, he had no shoes.

"Your feet are as ugly as ever," Joe said. They laughed together in pure joy.

"How is this possible?" Joe asked.

"No clue," Will said. Joe was squinting his eyes.

"I see others with you but can't quite make em all out," Joe said.

"Who is with you?" he asked.

Will said, "They're all here, all our fishermen buddies

who left before you. Not all can see you, it appears--don't know why. Like me, they wander the beach. Never know when we are coming or going."

"I have seen this young lady several times in the last few weeks," Will stated. "I think weeks, not sure cause I have lost all sense of time."

Lilly was watching Joe's facial expressions, trying to read the emotion. Meanwhile Rosie, Char and Henry were visiting with the other spirits. It was as if they were just stopping by for coffee. Brothers meeting up for a family reunion. This was new for Henry. At the wall it was nothing like this. These were men of his kind, his generation.

Lilly looked at Charlotte and smiled.

"I am so glad you're back," said Lilly. "I was worried I would never see you again." Lilly reached out to grab hold of Charlotte's hands.

"I can sense someone else is with you, but I can't see anyone. Is there someone else?"

"Yes," Charlotte announced, "my husband Henry is with me. He is here next to me. I put the sapphire ring on that he made for me and next thing I know I am in the house where he is at."

"The ring," Lilly said," he made the ring for you? Huh... what are the odds of that, girl?" Lilly instantly remembered what she had read in the old book about the island that once housed tradesmen, the island that is no more. She could not believe what she was hearing.

Lilly smiled. "I am so happy for you; in some odd way you are now together." Lilly was thinking in her head. Yep, my book is definitely going to be fiction; no one is going to believe this story.

Lilly sat down next to Joe, "You okay, Joe?" she asked.

"Yes, yes, I'm trying to take all this in."

"So, you've been here all this time seeing this? You must have been scared out of your wits."

"I was at first, but the more I came to the Point and got to know these women and listened to their story I became intrigued," Lilly said. "I wanted to know more. I felt a part of them. I don't understand why they're here, why other spirits come and go while they seem to be stuck here."

"Joe, we have to keep this to ourselves or the Point will become a shit show, okay?" Lilly said.

"This will be our secret," he said.

CHAPTER 34

Man bun, noun: a man's hairstyle in which the hair is drawn back into a tight coil at the back or top of the head.

Lilly disembarked the ferry thinking how fast the time had gone by. She couldn't wait to get her laptop fired up and start her book. Excited and sad at the same time, she was leaving the Point and her new friends. Taking a deep breath, she sighed as if she had just landed on another planet. Her mind was racing. How could she go back to a normal life as if nothing had happened? Like always, she would find a way to press on. The garage door opened and swallowed her into what once was.

In some small way it was nice to be back home. Maybe some normalcy would be good.

She poured herself a glass of wine and turned the radio on. An Al Green song started to play. Lilly began unpacking her bag, pulling out dirty t-shirts, holding them up to her nose to see if she could get one more whiff of the sea air.

"Smells like old sweat, with a hint of low tide," she said as she tossed them onto a pile on the floor.

"What's this?" An old blue cloth napkin was wadded up and tied with a piece of brown twine. Lilly recognized the napkin from Rosie's tea table. She sat on the floor and slowly, carefully untied the bow twine. Inside, a piece of paper was folded up. Lilly opened the letter, written in beautiful cursive writing, deep black ink she began to read.

Dearest Lilly,

You're probably wondering how I was able to write this letter. I got some help. It's my secret how I got these words on paper. If you are reading this, you are probably back home. In this old napkin are the old coins and jewels from the wooden box. Here is what we want you to do with these treasures...

Tears welled up in her eyes as she finished unfolding the napkin and saw the coins and the jewels.

"How the hell did these get in here?" she whispered. The old jewels had been polished a bit but the coins were as she had seen them originally. Old, worn and weathered. She folded the napkin back up and held the bundle against her chest. Lilly couldn't sleep that night, sorting through her thoughts and the next plan of action. In the morning she would hop in the car and drive to Manhattan.

Lilly pulled up to the old building. She had heard this museum was well known for historic knowledge and for the resources the large library contained. "Here it is," she said aloud. Leaning forward toward the dashboard she held a small piece of paper with the museum address. She approached the parking lot. The old man with a bright orange vest said, "Park on the east side and enter through the green door."

There was the door, just like he said. Unbuckling her seat belt, she grabbed her bag, this building obviously had been here for a long time. White daisies graced the walkway, a simple reassurance. Lilly's favorite flower.

"I hope I'm doing the right thing," she whispered.

"Here goes nothing." Lilly opened the old green door, a reminder of the library back at the Point. A sign on the wall posted: Curator/historian with an arrow indicating to continue forward.

"Here it is, room 503," said Lilly.

Lilly entered and was greeted by what appeared to be a student, young, obviously working on some kind of school paper.

Hello, I have an appointment with Mr. Sundance. My name is Lilly, Lilly Smith."

"Yes, have a seat," said the student. "I will let Mr. Sundance know you're here."

Lilly couldn't help but notice the artifacts, relics everywhere hanging on the walls. Photographs of places she had never seen. Everything looked strategically placed with care. Some earned the honor of a wall lamp. Lilly raised her eyebrows and thought for a second. She sure wouldn't want to be the one to have to dust this place. Just then a gentleman entered the lobby.

"Hello, Ms. Smith, I'm Charles Sundance," he said as he reached out his hand. "Nice to meet you."

"Hello, thanks for seeing me today," Lilly replied.

"Come into my office and let's visit," said Charles. Charles was not as old as she thought he might be for a curator. He was tall, slender, brown hair with a peppering of gray. On the back of his head was a man bun. Lilly wondered what possessed a grown man to have a man bun. Lilly thought he was good-looking, beautiful green eyes, maybe in his late fifties wearing a Bob Marley t-shirt. She had a good feeling about Charles. Following him into the large office, she found herself slightly annoyed. His hair looked better than hers, which forced her to fluff up her hair a bit while he was not looking.

The large room had a table in the center. It was high, made of old barn wood with stacks of papers, books and several pencil holders.

"Here, you can lay out what you have and let's take a look," said Charles. He laid out a white rolled up cloth and retrieved his glasses, as well as a magnifying glass that sat on a stand. Her hands started to shake as she began to unwrap the napkin. Charles noticed and gently pressed his hand on hers and said, "Don't worry, I've been doing this for years. I promise if you have something here, we will become good friends."

Lilly let out a sigh, "It's just that these items carry meaning to me, and I hope by coming here I am doing the right thing."

He nodded. "I understand." Putting his glasses on and tilting his head back he leaned over to get a closer look. His first reach was the coins. He kept getting closer and closer flipping them over, squinting his eyes. He stood up, grabbed a note pad and pencil and started jotting down the year on each coin. At one point he put the paper over a coin, and with a pencil rubbed the imprint of the coin the same way she had done not so long ago.

"What do you think?" Lilly asked. He stood up, took his glasses off and asked, "Where did you get these coins?"

Lilly said, "They have been in my family, where they came from is my secret." She suddenly looked the slightest bit stern.

"These coins are definitely rare; I know someone who would love to take a look at them if that's okay with you?" he asked. Charles leaned in again to take another look. "The jewelry–now that is my expertise." Charles stood up, tilted his head to the right a bit. He went over to one of the many shelves that lined the walls. There must have been over five thousand books that fenced the room.

"I actually know where to find most of the books in this room," he said. "This book in particular, I have not pulled out in a long time."

Lilly watched him scan the room. He raised his hand, like a divining rod to retrieve the correct book, a titanic of binders.

"Here it is!" he said.

"This book here is an artifact in itself." He lifted the old book and brought it to the table.

"Wait," Lilly said. "I know this book." She placed her hand on the hard cover, feeling the seasoned leather. This is the same book she had looked in at the old library, only this one appeared to be the original. The book had the musty smell and character she loved so much, the crunchy pages. Lilly did not want to announce where she had seen the other book.

Quickly she backed off and made up a story about seeing the same book online while researching. With a slight grin, she wondered how long it would take bun man to figure out what he was looking for was on page 911?

"Manor Island, I think the jewelry is from a small island called Manor Island," Charles said. "There was a particular tradesman discovered many years ago. I am an expert on his work, back in college I did extensive research about this island," he said.

"If I can confirm this, you definitely have something here—almost priceless," Charles stated.

Lilly headed straight to open a safe deposit box at a nearby bank. After she deposited the items for safekeeping, she stood in the lobby, wondering how her life was about to change.

CHAPTER 35

Football game: played on a 100-yard field with two teams of 11 players and one goal at each end.

Charlotte and Rosie were once again out on the sand dunes.

"No one on the beach today--just us," Charlotte said. Rosie was picking the dirt out of her fingernails. Like always, the wind was blowing, the sea grass was stretching, and the tide withdrawing for the evening. Henry joined them, sitting next to Charlotte with a grin.

"I had forgotten what this place looked like, what it felt like, the fishy saltiness of low tide," he said. Henry picked up a small stone from the sand, rubbed it in the palm of his hands.

"I would like to build a stone wall like the one where I came from. What do you ladies think, are you okay with it?" asked Henry.

Charlotte smiled and said, "I think it's a lovely idea."

"Rosie, what do you say?" Henry asked.

"Only if you let me help build it," she said.

Henry stood and looked around, "We will need to find just the right spot, start out small. Maybe, once the wall is ready, we can get Lilly to spread the word, you know, about the wall. She could write an article in the local newspaper."

Charlotte looked down the beach and wondered when she would see Lilly again. Had she read the letter and what was she doing if anything with the items from the old wooden box?

"First thing tomorrow, we'll find a good spot for your so-called wall; right now it's teatime," Rosie said.

Morning came and Henry had already found a spot for the new wall, a small area protected by the sturdy lighthouse. Soon Rosie was outside collecting stones, telling Henry how to stack them. He just gave her a grin.

"Large ones on the bottom for stability need to be sturdy against the wind's gusts," he said. It would take them several days to get the wall built and another several days to make sure it was solid. Already, birds were stopping by, checking out a new resting place to perch.

The wall was about twenty-five feet long and three feet high tucked away so if anyone came to the lighthouse, they would not notice it–for now anyway. For a brief moment sunbeams filtered down through the clouds as if to say, well done.

Today, there was a visitor to the beach, a spirit visitor –a man, heavy set wearing shorts and a t-shirt with N.Y. on the front, dark, grayish hair with a kind smile. As he drew closer it was obvious he saw the three residents of the beach.

"Hello," Henry said. "Are you just passing through?"

The stranger said, "I don't know, I don't know where I am," he said.

"You are at the Point," Charlotte said. "Don't worry you're one of many spirits who pass through here. You are welcome to stay as long as you like."

Rosie asked, "Are you okay?"

"I'm a bit confused, I was on my couch watching a football game and that is all I remember," he said.

"How long have you been here?" the man asked.

Rosie piped up, "Not sure really and I don't know what a football game is. We have read bits and pieces of such from newspapers that have blown down the beach." The man looked around up and down the beach.

"There is something about this place, like I've been here before, just something peaceful about it. I can't place it."

"Do you mind if I sit for a while?" he asked.

"Sit as long as you like," replied Rosie.

CHAPTER 36

Millionaire (mil'ye ner) noun: a person whose wealth comes to at least a million dollars.

Lilly wrapped up the last of her wine glasses and gently placed them in a box. She had lived in this house for twenty plus years. She stood there looking around as the moving company loaded the last of the cartons. The red SOLD sign in the front lawn was confirmation. She stood there with a deep sigh, a breath of new beginnings. She felt sad and excited all at the same time. She made sure the front door was locked and watched as the moving truck drove away.

"This is it," she murmured, "let's do this." Lilly threw her oversized purse in the front seat, rolled the windows down and headed for the ferry.

A John Denver song was playing on the radio: perfect. She reached for the dial to turn it up. Soon she was sitting on the ferry among strangers. Thinking back she recalled the last time she rode the ferry, the mother-daughter conversation, the old man and his awful tube socks.

Lilly was excited to see Charlotte and Rosie but yet also a bit hesitant. What if they were no longer on the Point after all these months? What if they had moved on like the others who just passed through. Either way Lilly was excited and couldn't wait to get to the island and the lighthouse.

Finally docked, Lilly drove off the ferry and headed straight to the Point. Main Street looked the same--warm and inviting. She rolled her window down as she drove past the bread shop hoping to get a whiff of todays special. The library's double doors were wide open, and she caught a glimpse of someone sweeping the floor. Was there a warm pot of Arabica coffee brewing inside? She loved the fact that she felt a part of the town and knew where its heritage was grounded.

The lighthouse parking lot was an inviting sight. The first thing that caught her eye was a new sign about the parking restrictions. This one was now metal instead of wood. Must have figured this would stand up to any gusts of wind. Lilly bent down, picked up a small stone, threw it at the sign, and heard the loud ping. With a grin on her face, she put her sweater on, threw her shoes on the floor of the car and headed toward the lighthouse.

Today the sky was a bit hazy, windy with a few white-caps. Typical, beautiful beach day. The wind on her face felt like the cosmos was drawing her in. The tall brown grass-es were waving hello. The sand on her feet felt wonderful again. As she drew closer to the lighthouse, she squinted a bit. Had anyone noticed she was here? She decided she'd sit in her old favorite spot, her spot that had been transformed a bit over the months. She waited. Where were the ladies of the Point--was Henry still here?

Charlotte came up from behind Lilly and slowly walked around to see if it was really her in the brown sweater.

"Charlotte," Lilly said, "you're here!" holding her hand against her chest. I was so worried I would never see you again. Charlotte sat down with a big smile. Lilly asked, "Is Rosie here...Henry?

"Yes, yes, we are all still here." It didn't take long before Rosie appeared.

"Well, girl, it's nice to see your face again, what you been up to?" Rosie asked with her mock-stern voice.

"Well, ladies, I found the napkin you left me in my suitcase. I couldn't believe it; how did you do that?" Lilly asked.

"Never you mind," Rosie said. "Did you make good use of it or is it still wrapped up in that old napkin?"

Lilly began to tell her story about how she'd taken the items to a historian and how the gentleman there was familiar with the island, Manor Island. He knew about the jeweler who lived there and had studied the residents. He knew the history of the time, who lived there, what was bought and sold. He even had a logbook of goods sold. I saw Henry's name in the log and next to it listed under purchased items was a blue sapphire ring. It was amazing. I visited this guy several times. I called him 'bun man' because he had a bun on his head."

Eyes tilted, Rosie said, "Was it like a woman's bun?"

"Yes, a bun." Lilly reached to the back of her head as if to describe where a man would put such a thing. Lilly said, "a man bun," lifting her eyebrows. "Anyway, I visited him over a dozen times, keeping the items in a safe deposit box all the while. I couldn't bear to leave the items with anyone else."

Lilly also told them about how she kept it a secret where the items came from and how she'd reported that the items were passed down in the family.

"I have completely renovated and sold my old house with some of the money I made from the items." Looking cautious, she said, "I hope it was okay to sell some of the coins."

"Of course," Charlotte said, "that's what we wanted you to do! We wanted some good to come out of this. And we were hoping you would move to the island here close to the Point."

Tears began to roll down Lilly's cheeks, "That's exactly what I've done. I purchased a home down the road with a beautiful view of the beach and a perfect view of the lighthouse—I want to show hospitality. I quit my job; shit, I will never have to work again. I want to write a book–a book about you and this place if that's okay."

I will change the location, of course, so you don't get besieged by hero worshippers."

Charlotte also had tears on her face. "That is wonderful that you moved. We can be together now."

With a smile on her face, Rosie asked, "How much did you get for the coins?"

Lilly smiled, wiping the tears and said, "One hundred and seventeen million dollars! And I didn't even sell it all. I was hoping we could find a charity to donate some of the money."

Lilly stretched out her right hand, "Here, ladies, these are two rings from the box. Small circles of sapphires, placed in silver bands. I had them cleaned up and reset as closely to the original item as possible. I still have some other jewelry and coins as well. I just could not give it all up, not now anyway."

By this time Henry joined the conversation. "I remember the logbook the jeweler had. He said it had pages and pages of items listed. I remember thinking he had a good business going," Henry said.

"I have other news," Lilly said. "Sounds like the townspeople have requested the lighthouse be functional again. Have you noticed if anyone else has been by looking over the lighthouse?"

"Yes, Henry said, "a nice fellow, seemed like he really cared about the structure of the lighthouse. He even noticed our recent stone wall. Come, take a look, Lilly."

Lilly followed Henry around to the side of the lighthouse. "Looks like it should have always been here," said Lilly.

"I would like to be one of the first to add a note if you don't mind," she said. Henry just gave her a grin and a nod.

Lilly explained there was going to be a town meeting in a few days to decide what would happen to the lighthouse. "There might be an active keeper living here," she said.

The town hall building was just like you'd see in an old movie. The seats were old, made of wood that folded up when no one was sitting. The usual musty smell pervaded. The hall was packed with some familiar faces. Lilly rubbed her hand across the top of the bench before she sat. If these seats could talk.

Lilly had a sense there were others in the room, none of whom were living. She gazed around and could see shadows, filters of dust moving about, cold drafts. It comforted her to know spirits were there among the living. Lilly tried to read the living--could anyone else sense what she could?

After a few introductions, a few readings of notes, the meeting started.

"Hello, my name is August Long," he said. "I am an engineer and I would like to be the keeper of your lighthouse." He went on to explain his credentials and that he recently retired. Lilly thought he seemed kind and handsome. He expressed how he cared for the old lighthouse. He went on to tell the story about how his great, great, great grandfather was once the keeper and lived nearby the lighthouse. He had done extensive research on it. It was a great comfort to Lilly to know he cared. She couldn't stomach the thought of someone in the lighthouse who didn't treasure it as much as she did.

Two weeks later it was decided August was now the lighthouse keeper. The town voted to allow August to build a residence back from the lighthouse.

CHAPTER 37

Home (hom) noun: the place where a person (or family) lives.

Lilly approached the small rugged stone wall. She pulled out of her pocket a folded up note, held it to her lips for a moment, closed her eyes, and took a deep breath before she found just the right spot for the note to her brother. Just then a dark-haired man with a kind smile, shorts and t-shirt appeared again. A spirit. Lilly's brother, Rob. He bent down in the sand next to Lilly.

"Can she see me?" he asked.

Lilly looked up and turned her head. "I love you, Rob. Oh, how I've missed you" she whispered.

"Well, I'm here now and I probably ain't leaving."

It had been three months since the town hall meeting. August was well into the construction of his simple house. Lilly had been to the Point several times to visit with her friends. Strangely Charlotte, Rosie and Henry were nowhere to be found. Word had gotten out about the small wall and notes left to those who have departed. Every time Lilly visited the wall, more and more notes and trinkets appeared.

Coins, beaded bracelets, bells, padlocks with no keys. She often wondered what Henry would have thought about the objects left behind.

"Hello Lilly," said August. "Back again?"

"Yes, this place is very special to me; it's the reason I moved here," Lilly said. "This is now my home."

August pointed upward. "I need to do a few repairs up in the light. Care to join me?

"Yes, I would love that," Lilly replied. As she walked up the spiral staircase slowly, a flood of memories came to mind. She walked slowly with her hands against the rough brick as if she could feel the lighthouse breathing. The spot where the wooden box was hidden now appeared to have been sealed up with new cement. August must have made the repair. Finally at the top, looking around, she saw that the small table and table cloth was gone. Just an empty room. Lilly wondered if Charlotte and Rosie were able to move on because there was a new resident at the light.

August pulled open his tool chest. Have you been up here before?" he asked.

"Yes, I have many times," she said. "But every time I come up here, I am still in awe of the view." Lilly opened the glass door and stepped outside.

"Be careful there," August said, "a bit windy up here."

Lilly looked off into the distance, the small pier. The wind was whipping her hair about. Squinting her eyes, she saw the sky was dark, ready to release its wrath.

"Looks like someone is out there," she whispered. It was Charlotte waving and just like that she was gone.

Three years passed after Lilly moved to Beach Road. Lilly and August had become an item, enjoying each other's company, enjoying the Point. August was the first to read her recently published book. He understood her love for the lighthouse and the stone wall with notes. Lilly's book became a best seller. She loved seeing the book displayed in the bookstore window on Main Street. Henry left behind his old leather bound copies of all the notes. This would be the inspiration for her next book.

Just before a foggy dawn one morning, Lilly went to the top of the lighthouse with a mug of rich coffee and two oatmeal raisin cookies. Gazing out to the point, she glimpsed no one. Lilly turned around to step back inside the glass dome, and there, smudged in the glass condensation someone had formed the letters "H&C".

End (end): noun the reason for being final.